John S. Watson

The Life of George Fox

Founder of the Quakers - fully and impartially

John S. Watson

The Life of George Fox
Founder of the Quakers - fully and impartially

ISBN/EAN: 9783337332655

Printed in Europe, USA, Canada, Australia, Japan

Cover: Foto ©Andreas Hilbeck / pixelio.de

More available books at **www.hansebooks.com**

Life of George Fox,

THE FOUNDER OF THE QUAKERS.

FULLY AND IMPARTIALLY RELATED ON THE AUTHORITY OF HIS
OWN JOURNAL AND LETTERS, AND THE HISTORIANS
OF HIS OWN SECT.

BY THE

Rev. John Selby Watson,

M.A., M.R.S.L.

Hinc atque illinc humeros ad vulnera durat.—VIRG.
O'er bog, or steep, through strait, rough, dense, or rare.—MILT.

LONDON:
SAUNDERS, OTLEY, AND CO.,
CONDUIT STREET.
1860.

PREFACE.

THE chief object with which the following Life of George Fox has been written is to show how much may be effected by the resolute perseverance of one man, notwithstanding opposition, danger, insult, ridicule, and vexation of every kind. The narrative is not intended either to favour the Quakers, or to throw undue contempt or censure on them. It simply relates the fortunes of their founder, as they appear in his own pages, or in those of the historians of his sect; the principal authorities for what is told being George Fox's own journal and letters, and the histories of Croese, Sewel, and Gough.

Of Fox's assistant preachers few notices are introduced, for the adventures of each of them so nearly resemble those of their leader, that to tell his story renders it unnecessary to tell theirs. All adopted George's tenets, and all suffered similar persecution for the dissemination of them.

It has not been thought necessary to encumber the pages with references, for the books from which the matter is taken may be easily consulted by such as wish to examine them, and the public may be assured that nothing is here stated for which the writings of Fox or his followers do not furnish ample authority.

J. S. W.

CONTENTS.

Contents.

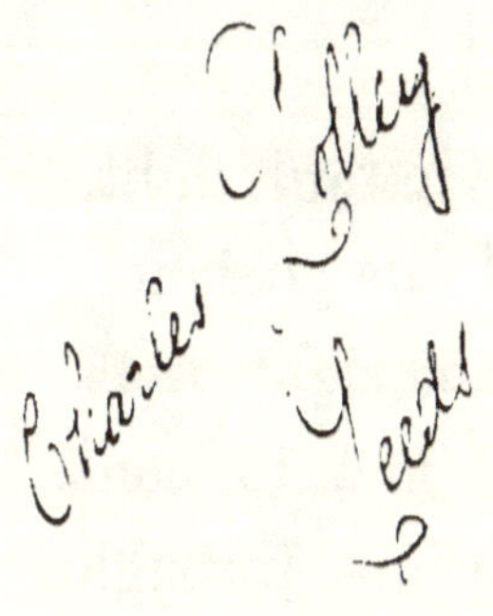

Life of George Fox.

CHAPTER I.

Introductory. Peculiarities of the Quakers.

BEFORE I relate the life of George Fox, it may be proper to give some account of the tenets and practices of the sect of which he was the founder. The reasons why they hold these tenets, and observe these practices, will be but slightly noticed at present, but will become fully apparent in the course of the following biography.

The great principle on which all their belief rests is, that every human being is

B

endowed with a portion of inward light, by which, if he duly attend to its guidance, he is enabled to distinguish right from wrong, and good from evil, and to conduct himself properly in his course through life. This light men receive, they say, from Christ, who, as it is expressed in the beginning of St. John's Gospel, "lighteth every man that cometh into the world."

Considering that every man has thus a spiritual communication, through Christ, from God, they assert that all intercourse between man and God must be solely of a spiritual nature; that worship offered to God must be solely an emanation from the heart of man, and cannot be assisted, nor ought any attempts to be made to assist it, by external objects or sounds. All religious ceremonies, therefore, they regard as not only useless, but as obstructive, to purity of worship, since they divert the attention from the suggestions of the light or grace within. Hence they admit no forms of prayer, or regular sermons, nor consider any place to be necessarily devoted to religious service, which may be performed anywhere, they believe, with equal effect. They do not neglect, however, to meet together for the purpose of mutual exhortation; but when they assemble, they sit down in silence, till some one conceives himself moved by the spirit within him to address the rest; and he then declares to them such thoughts as he believes to be the offspring of his own mind.

Since this internal stimulus is necessary to all exhortation of others, it follows that it is superfluous to select particular individuals as preachers, or to educate particular persons for the office of the ministry. Men receive the Gospel freely, and they are to communicate it freely, and of themselves, without looking to any human instruction

or authority for support or approbation.
All that is done, of a religious nature,
for the community, is to be voluntary and
gratuitous; a paid priesthood is an order
of men not to be tolerated.

Even the two great rites, Baptism and
the Eucharist, which are so much regarded
by other Christians, the one as the means
of initiation into the church of Christ, the
other as the means of maintaining communion with Him, they pronounce, from
the entire spirituality of their belief, to be
unessential; for they conceive that men
become true members of Christ's mystical
body by faith in Him, and by cherishing
within them the light with which He
endows them, without the intervention of
water or any other outward instrument or
sign; and that communion with Him is
maintained and secured by the same means,
the true Lord's Supper being that intimated in the Revelation, " Behold, I stand

at the door and knock; if any man hear my voice, and open the door, I will come in to him, and sup with him, and he with me."

They hold it to be their duty to strive after absolute freedom from sin, and to make themselves perfect, as far as may be possible, even as God is perfect; and when they address others, who are not of their community, they impress upon them the necessity of repenting of their sins that they have committed, and of total abstinence from sin for the time to come.

They do not receive the doctrine of the Trinity, for they do not admit the personality of the Holy Ghost; their creed being, in this respect, that there is one God, that Christ is his Son, and that the Holy Spirit is but an emanation from God, which He uses as an instrument to influence the minds of men.

Since God made all human beings of

one blood, and is no respecter of persons, they consider that women, in all religious points of view, are to be regarded as on an entire equality with men, and are to be allowed the same freedom in addressing congregations.

As men are exhorted in the Scriptures to love one another, even their enemies, the Quakers do not acknowledge the lawfulness of war, or of any kind of bloodshed or revenge, but think it the duty of all to forgive such as have injured them, and to oppose injustice and oppression only with patience.

The Scriptural admonition that men's yea should be yea, and their nay, nay, and the exhortation "Swear not at all," they regard as enjoining all men to speak the truth unequivocally, and as prohibiting not only false and profane swearing, but all oaths of all kinds. They feel bound to speak truth individually, and they deem, not merely that there is no necessity for oaths, but that it would be a reproach to their veracity to assert it by swearing, even in a court of justice, yet expressing their readiness, if they are found guilty of falsehood in their words, to submit to the same punishment for it as others suffer for perjury.

As Christianity was designed to detach men from the world, and to raise them above it, they affirm it to be wrong to use titles of honour, flattering gestures, or compliments of respect, which are mere worldly follies and vanities, and foster that pride in the heart which ought to be eradicated from it. They therefore abstain from taking off the hat as a mark of obeisance, and from addressing any one as " your majesty" or " your excellency," or by any other similar designation. They use the pronouns " thou " and " thee," in speaking to any single person; a practice which they the more readily adopted, as, when Quakerism arose, the plural "you" was often addressed to a rich person, and the singular "thou" to a poor one.

The same simplicity which they observed in their language, they adopted also in their dress and mode of living. The apparel both of men and women was to be of the plainest material and colour, all gaudy and superfluous ornaments being laid aside. Their houses were to be embellished neither with painting nor sculpture, which, even when employed on the best of subjects, were but means, they considered, of fostering the love of ostentation. They were to abstain from music, singing, and dancing, and never to be present either at theatres, concerts, or parties of amusement, which would lead to worldly acquaintanceship and worldly corruption, and detach the mind from those serious subjects which demanded its whole attention.

The establishment of such a system of life was not to be effected without much energy and obstinacy on the part of those who commenced it. Being so much at variance with the general feelings and notions of mankind, it was sure to meet with opposition and hostility from every side. Almost every custom and practice of society, and every profession and employment, except that of the mere tradesman, would be in some degree affected and debilitated by it. Not only would the church suffer, but the occupations of the army and navy, and of all who live by the love of litigation in their neighbours, and subtle interpretations of the law, would be at end. Even kingly power might soon be reduced to a nullity; for what would be the authority of a ruler over a nation of

Quakers, who maintained that all men were equal, and of whom none showed any token of deference to his neighbour, but each thought himself as well qualified to govern as any of those around him?

The sect has been, for some time, not at all on the increase, for whatever is opposed to the common sense of mankind will gradually fall to decay; but that it made such sudden and rapid progress at its rise, and that it was inspired with such vitality as to last so large a number of years, was owing to the zeal and resolution of one man, who was deterred from maintaining whatever he was determined to advocate as right, by no obstacles, intimidations, or perils, and whose actions and fortunes I shall now proceed to relate.

CHAPTER II.

GEORGE FOX was born some time in the month of July, in the year 1624, at Drayton in the Clay in Leicestershire. His parents, Christopher and Mary, were members of the Church of England. His father was a weaver, and so honest a man that his neighbours called him Righteous Christer. His mother's maiden name was Lago, and she was of a family in which there had been martyrs.

He was remarkable, from his earliest years, for such a gravity and sedateness of mind as is seldom seen in children; and, whenever he saw older persons conducting themselves loosely and improperly, used to say to himself, as he tells us in his Journal, "surely when I become a man, my behaviour will not resemble theirs."

He was a boy of few words, and extremely observant of truth. He cared little for childish plays, and made a resolution to eat and drink only so much as was requisite to support nature.

He was carefully brought up by his mother, by whom he was taught to read; and he afterwards learned to write, though but in a poor way; nor was his reading ever very far extended.

As he grew up, and showed such solemnity of demeanour, some of his relatives were inclined to have him educated for a clergyman; but others objected to this course, and eventually had him apprenticed to a shoemaker, who also dealt in wool, and had some land on which he grazed cattle.

Of all the employments that his master assigned him, he took most pleasure in tending sheep, in which he became very skilful. His master, while George was with him, was extremely prosperous. In his dealings with others, George often used the word " verily," and it was a common saying among those that knew him, that if George said " verily," nothing would make him depart from his word. If boys or others laughed at him, he paid little heed to their jibes; while with people in general his innocence and candour rendered him a favourite.

About this time commenced the civil war between the royal and parliamentary forces; a war in which religion was not without its share; for many of the bishops had irritated the people by the introduction of innovation into the services of the church. One of these, which caused particular dissatisfaction, was the ceremony of the priest's bowing thrice when he approached the communion-table, which began to be termed the high-altar. Other ceremonies were added from time to time; and such preachers were most favoured by the bishops as showed most inclination to High-church proceedings, or rather to popery. Endeavours were made, too, to force episcopacy on the people of Scotland, and this served to increase the tendency to rebellion throughout both countries. War became at length unavoidable, Charles raised the royal standard at Nottingham, in the month of August, 1642; and in the same year was fought the indecisive battle of Edgehill, in which, but for the rash impetuosity of Prince Rupert, the parliamentary forces, under the Earl of Essex, might have been defeated.

While the minds of men, from these causes, were in the highest state of excitement, it happened that George Fox, now in the nineteenth year of his age, being at a fair in his part of the country, was asked by a cousin of his, named Bradford, whom he calls a professor, and another man of the same stamp, to drink part of a jug of beer with them; a request with which George, who was thirsty, and who liked the company of professors, readily complied. But when they had drunk a glass each, the two professors began to drink healths, and, observing some reluctance in George to fraternize with them, called for more drink, and declared that he who would not drink the healths that they proposed should pay the whole reckoning. George was grieved at this denunciation, and having never been called upon, as he tells us, either by professors or others, to drink healths before, determined not to yield to the custom on the present occasion. He therefore took out a groat, laid it on the table for his share of the cost, and quitted the company.

It would appear that the propriety of drinking healths, in which ordinary men see no harm, had been already denied by some of the stricter sectarians as a practice vain, heathenish, and of evil tendency, provoking people to drink to excess. Questions about ceremonies in the church had led men to consider the good or evil, the lawfulness or unlawfulness, of the most ordinary doings of common life; and many saw impiety in acts that were totally innoxious. George Fox discerned such enormity in wishing health to a fellow-creature over a draught of ale that he wondered how any that professed a sense of religion could be guilty of it.

When he went home, he could not go to sleep, or to bed, but walked up and down his room during the night, often praying and crying to the Lord, who, as he imagined, replied to his supplications with this admonition, "Thou seest how young people go together into vanity, and old people fix their thoughts on the earth; thou must therefore forsake all, both young and old, and be as a stranger to all."

This command, as he believed it to be, made such an impression on his mind, that he resolved to break off intimate communion and fellowship with all, even his own relations, and to live a solitary life. Accordingly, on the 9th of September, 1643, he left his home at Drayton, and went to Lutterworth, from whence, after a stay of some time, he removed to Northampton, where he also made some stay, and then went to Newport-Pagnel, in Buckinghamshire. Hence he travelled to Barnet, which he entered in the month of June, 1644.

During his progress through the country, he did not so entirely abstain from intercourse with others, but that he came in contact, by whatever means, with several professors, who noticed him, and sought to become acquainted with him; but he found no pleasure in their company, as he considered that they " did not possess what they professed." He began at the same time, too, to feel some distrust of himself, and to doubt whether he had done right in forsaking his relations. He had at times strong feelings of despair, and wondered why such trouble came upon him. He believed that Satan was laying snares for him, and was bent on tempting him to commit some grievous sin, that he might be sunk into hopeless despondency. He meditated over all that he had done in his past life, and was unable to discover why it should be thus with him; but it was some consolation to him to reflect that Christ himself had been tempted. He sometimes shut himself in his chamber, and sometimes wandered solitary in the woods, waiting for spiritual communica-

tions; but his troubles of mind still continued, nor was he freed from them, he
says, for many years, though he applied
to numbers of persons for spiritual comfort.

CHAPTER III.

At length he went from Barnet to London, and took a lodging there, hoping that some of the great professors of that city would be able to afford him advice and relief; but he found all to whom he went greatly in the dark. One of those to whom he addressed himself was an uncle of his, named Pickering, a Baptist, who introduced him to others of that persuasion, which was then but in its infancy, and all appear to have received him kindly;

yet he could not resolve to open his mind to them, or to become one of their number, for what he saw in them did not please him. Being thus dissatisfied, he determined to go back again into Leicestershire; a determination which he was the more willing to adopt, as he heard that his parents and relations were troubled at his absence, and was desirous to diminish their grief by letting them see that he was unharmed.

When he arrived at home, his relations were desirous to prevent him from roving by prevailing on him to marry; but George told them that he was yet a lad, and must get wisdom before he assumed the cares of matrimony. They would then have enlisted him in the train-bands of the Parliament, who were now successfully opposing the King, but George had no mind for a military life, and professed himself of too tender a constitution to encounter

the hardships of the field. He then left
home again, and went to Coventry, where
he took a room at the house of a professor,
and grew acquainted with a great many
people who were endeavouring to live re-
ligiously. But, being still restless and
discontented, he returned once more to Drayton, and continued there a year, suffering
great sorrows and troubles, and walking
many nights by himself.

From what source he obtained money
to support him in his peregrinations is
not known, but it appears, from his own
testimony, that he had enough to prevent
him from being chargeable to those about
him, and was able to administer occasionally to other people's necessities.

During his stay at Drayton he was
often visited by the vicar of the place,
Nathaniel Stevens, to whom he also
often went himself, and sometimes found
another priest with him, both of whom

would often ask him questions, and listen attentively to his answers. One day Stevens asked him, why Christ cried out upon the cross, "My God, why hast thou forsaken me?" and prayed that, if it was possible, this cup might pass from Him.

George answered, as might have been expected, that Christ uttered those words under the pressure of the sins of all mankind, which his human nature was scarcely able to bear. Stevens applauded the answer as something more than ordinary, and afterwards spoke highly of George to others. But George subsequently found that Stevens led him to speak during the week-days on subjects on which he intended to preach on the Sundays; hence George conceived a lower opinion of him. Dislike arose on both sides, and Stevens at length became George's great persecutor.

He then went to another clergyman at Manchester, and asked him for some instructions as to the causes of despair and temptations; but he, regarding George as a weak enthusiast, bade him smoke tobacco and sing psalms. George replied, that he hated tobacco, and was too despondent to sing; the priest then said that he might come again another day, and he would tell him several things; but when George went, he found him in an ill humour, and discovered that he had made a jest of his troubles to his servants, so that even the milk-maids were ready to laugh at him; and George was grieved that he had opened his mind to so indiscreet a person.

Another priest at Tamworth, whom he consulted, he found but an empty hollow cask. He then heard favourable mention of a Dr. Cradock of Coventry, to whom he immediately went, and put to him the same questions as he had put to the priest at Manchester. A conversation began between them in the parsonage garden, where,

as they walked along one of the paths,
which was very narrow, George happened
to set his foot on a handsome flower-bed,
a trespass by which he enraged. Dr. Cradock, he says, as much as if he had set
his house on fire. Harmony was not likely
to be restored between them, and so George
came away with his trouble rather increased
than diminished.

The next priest to whom he applied
was named Macham, a man of some re-
pute, who thought that the best remedies
for George's disquietudes would be physic
and phlebotomy, which were accordingly
tried; but when they endeavoured to draw
blood from him, either in the arms or the
head, they found it impracticable, so tho-
roughly was his body dried up, he says,
with sorrow and grief. He could even
have wished never to have been born to
know the vanity or wickedness of mankind,
or to have been born blind, that he might

never have seen them, or deaf, that he might never have heard vain and wicked words.

Medical appliances having failed, he was left to go on his own way. He resumed his wanderings,' and, as he was walking in the fields one Sunday morning, in the early part of the year 1646, it was revealed to him by a light which arose within him, that to be bred at Oxford or Cambridge was not sufficient to qualify a man to be a minister of the Gospel. He was thus led to undervalue the services of the Church. He declined to attend the ministrations of the priest with his relations, but withdrew into the orchard or the fields with his Bible by himself; conduct at which his friends were much annoyed, but George endeavoured to pacify them by quoting the words of the Apostle, that "believers need no man to teach them, but as the anointing teacheth them."

This, they admitted, says George, to be
the language of Scripture, and to be true,
but they were, nevertheless, not satisfied.
However, he continued to hold aloof, not
only from Churchmen, but from Dissenters,
making himself strange to all, and relying
wholly on his own faith.

Soon after, it was revealed to him, by
the same light, that "God, who made
the world, dwells not in temples made
with hands." It might have been thought
that this text would have been quite
familiar to George, and that he would
have understood it in the sense intended,
that "He who pervades all things is not
confined to temples made with hands."
But George believed, or chose to believe,
that it was suggested to him in another sense,
indicating that God is positively absent
from men's temples, and dwells only in
men's hearts; that He did not dwell even
in Solomon's temple, which He Himself

commanded to be made, since He allowed it to be destroyed, but that He dwells in the hearts of his people, who exist always. George was highly elated with this discovery.

When he returned home, for he received this revelation also in the fields, he found that Stevens, the vicar, had been to his friends, and told them that he was afraid of him for going after new lights. George smiled, remembering what his inward light had told him respecting Stevens and his brethren. He did not, however, communicate the teachings of the light to his friends, for, "though they saw," says he, "beyond the priests, yet they went to hear them," and still continued to "grieve because I would not go also."

At this time he "had great openings," he says, "concerning the things written in the Revelation;" but when he spoke of his imaginations, the priests and professors would tell him that the Revelation was a sealed book, and advise him to think no more of it; but George used to tell them that Christ could open the seals, and that the things written in the book are the things nearest to us, for the Epistles were written to those who lived in former times, but the Revelation for those that should come after.

He fell in with some people that maintained that women have no souls. But George silenced them by citing the words of Mary, "My soul doth magnify the Lord."

He continued to suffer great troubles and temptations, but had, at the same time, "great openings of the Scripture," so that he exclaimed, he says, with David, though not exactly in David's sense of the words, "Day unto day uttereth speech, and night unto night sheweth knowledge."

When he had "openings," he says, they

answered one another, and answered the Scripture, and when he had troubles, they answered one another. What he means by these expressions is not very clear; for though we may imagine interpretations of texts, fanciful or sound, corresponding or answering to one another, and other passages of Scripture, yet we cannot easily conceive how he thought troubles answered one another. Sewel, who pays great attention to this part of George Fox's Journal, seems to think the passage unintelligible, for he passes it in silence.

CHAPTER IV.

George commences his travels through various parts
of England—His contemplations and resolutions—
His leather suit of apparel—He begins to teach
and preach, insisting on the necessity of a sinless
life—His farther internal revelations—He begins
to be followed.

GEORGE now travelled through parts of
Derbyshire, Leicestershire, and Nottinghamshire, meeting with some that repelled,
and others that listened to him. Among
those that paid him most attention was
Elizabeth Hooton, a woman of tender
conscience, who subsequently became dis-
tinguished among George's followers. But
as troubles still harassed him, he fasted
much, and wandered about in solitary
places for many days together with his

Bible, sheltering himself at night in hollow trees or other retreats. During this time he joined in no profession of religion with any, having taken leave of father and mother and all other relations, and considering himself a stranger in the earth; travelling up and down, which way soever he thought that the Lord inclined his heart; hiring a chamber for himself in any town to which he came; staying sometimes a month or more, and sometimes less, in a place; for he was afraid to stay too long anywhere, being suspicious alike of the professor and the profane, lest, by conversing much with either, he should be drawn from his purpose of seeking heavenly wisdom, and of endeavouring to transfer his affections wholly from worldly things to things above. His griefs were not without intermission, for he had occasional intervals of relief, when he at times felt such heavenly joy that he thought he had been in Abraham's bosom.

At this time he made himself, or caused to be made for him, a suit of clothes entirely of leather, not perhaps, as Croese says, because he could not forget his old connexion with leather when he was a shoemaker, but because he wanted strong apparel, which would suffer little in his peregrinations through the thickets, and put him to little expense in repairs.

Being convinced that to be bred at a University gave a man no title to be a priest, he paid little regard in his travels to the clergy of the Church, but turned his attention more towards the dissenting people, among whom, however, whether preachers or others, he found none, even of the most experienced, that could " speak to his condition." But when his hopes in them, and in all mankind, were gone, he seemed to hear a voice within him, saying, "There is One that can speak to thy condition;" and it was then revealed to him, by his internal light, why he had been reduced to such apparent helplessness, namely, that God might have all the glory. But externally he saw nothing but corruptions, and therefore entered into fellowship with no sort of people, seeking to have fellowship only with Heaven.. He persevered in the perusal of the Scriptures, which he wished to understand without any human aid, oral or written.

He heard of a woman in Lancashire that had fasted twenty-two days, and travelled to see her; but, when he came to her, found, he says, that she was under a temptation, and, having spoken to her what he had from the Lord, left her to the care of her father, who was one in high profession. Under what kind of temptation he supposed the woman to lie, and whether he thought that the temptation had enabled her really to fast twenty-two days, George does not say a syllable to enlighten us.

Soon after, as it appears, he made his first essay in preaching. On leaving the woman, he went, notwithstanding his dislike of communion with others, among the professors at Duckenfield and Manchester, where, to use his o w n words he "stayed a while, and declared truth, among them; and there were some convinced, who received the Lord's teaching, by which they were confirmed, and stood in the truth." But he offended the majority by insisting on the necessity of a sinless life, which they asserted to be unattainable in the imperfection of man's present condition.

About the same time there was a great meeting of the Baptists at Broughton in Leicestershire, at which were present also a number of people of other notions, and to which George found himself impelled to go. Here he tells us that the Lord again opened his mouth; that the everlasting truth was declared; that the Divine power began to spring; that he had great openings in the Scriptures; and that many were turned from darkness to light.

He then went into Nottinghamshire, where it was revealed to him by his inward light, what he might have discovered, it may be thought, without any illumination beyond that of other people, that the natures of those things which are hurtful without are to be found in the hearts of wicked men; for example, that in the breasts of the vicious are to be found the dispositions of dogs, swine, and vipers. He felt these tempers also in himself, and cried in his prayers, saying, " Why should I be thus? " Then it was revealed to him that it was necessary he should have a sense of all conditions, that he might address himself to all conditions with effect.

As he was walking in the town of Mansfield, it was declared to him by a Divine voice from within, "That which people trample upon must be thy food." He thought this, as any one else would have thought it, a very strange suggestion. But it was explained to him by the same Divine voice, at the same time, that the meaning was, that he must live by faith in Christ, upon which people trample while they feed one another with mere words. His monitor seems to have taken a needlessly circuitous way to exhort him to feed on faith.

His preaching now began to excite some attention, and people came from various quarters to hear him. He was fearful at first of being drawn too much from his contemplations by public exhibitions, but he felt himself internally urged to speak, and to open obscurities to the multitude. One Brown, too, who pretended to prophecy, had strong visions, he said, of George Fox on his death-bed, and declared that he would do great things, but that others, who were something only in show, would come to nothing. As soon as this Brown was dead, George says that *a great work of the Lord fell upon him*, and that he appeared, to the astonishment of many, as if he were dead, and, when he recovered, after about fourteen days, his body seemed to have been altered and new moulded. But while he was in this state, he had strong discernment given him, so that he saw into many who spoke very fluently of divine things, and perceived that it was merely the serpent that spoke in them. A report went abroad of him that he was a young man of a very discerning spirit, and many came from far and near, professors, priests, and people, to test the truth of the report; and George had "great openings and pro- phecies," so that his audience listened with wonder, and went away to spread his fame. Yet the tempter, in the midst of his glory, did not fail to pay him visits, and endeavoured to persuade him that he had sinned against the Holy Ghost; but George inquired in what par- ticular, and received no satisfactory answer; and, as he reflected that St. Paul, after he had been taken up into the third heaven, felt a messenger of Satan sent to buffet him, he became tolerably recon- ciled to his condition, and regarded the good as balancing the evil.

CHAPTER V.

THE King was now in the Isle of Wight.
He had sought refuge with the Scotch,
when they were besieging Newark, in May
of the preceding year; but they had soon
ceased to protect him, and had retired into
their own country on the promise of receiving four hundred thousand pounds as
arrears of pay. He had then been required
by the Parliament to reside at Holmby,
near Northampton; but from thence Cromwell's party forcibly removed him in June,

1647, and fixed him ultimately at Hampton Court, where the officers of the army entered into negotiation with him, and offered what might seem fair terms of accommodation. But Charles, while he was listening to their proposals, was treating, in his usual duplicity, with the opposite party; and, not feeling sure of the support of either side, became at length fearful for his personal safety, and at length effected his escape to the seaside, where he fell into the hands of Colonel Hammond, who confined him in Carisbrook Castle in November.

The two principal demands of the Parliament, in reference to religious affairs, were that the King should consent to the abolition of episcopacy, and the alienation of the bishops' lands; demands which he resolutely resisted.

During this state of things, large meetings were held in different parts of the country to consider of religious matters; and many such gatherings took place in Nottinghamshire, where George Fox then was. In the year 1648, there was a meeting of priests and professors at a justice's house, where George presented himself, and preached upon the saying of St. Paul that he had not known sin but by the law which said, " Thou shalt not covet." At another meeting, collected at Mansfield, he prayed, when the Divine power was so manifested that the house appeared to be shaken, and some remarked that it was as in the days of old, when the house was shaken where the apostles were. But when George had finished, one of the professors would pray; and his prayer was so dull that it made everything quiet again; and some of his brethren remonstrated with him, and told him that Satan must have tempted him to pray. The dull professor was then ashamed of himself, and asked George to pray again to reanimate them; but George replied that he could not pray for man's will.

Travelling through the country, he heard of a great meeting to be held at Leicester, at which were to be present Presbyterians, Independents, Baptists, and "Common-prayer men," to discuss some disputed points of doctrine. "The meeting was to be," says George, "in a steeple-house, and thither I was moved to go." The building was crowded; the priest was in the pulpit, and he gave every one present leave to speak. After some disputation, a woman asked the priest a question concerning regeneration, when he exclaimed,—

"I permit not a woman to speak in the church!"

At these words, George was stimulated, as in a rapture, to utterance, and immediately asked the priest,—

" Dost thou call this building a church?

or dost thou term this mixed multitude a church?"

But the priest replied to his questions by another,

"What is a church?"

"The Church," answered George, "is the pillar and ground of truth, made up of living stones and living members; a spiritual household, of which Christ is the Head; but He is not the Head of a mixed multitude, or of an old house composed of lime, stone, and wood."

This declaration excited much clamour; the priest came down from his pulpit, the people rushed from their pews; and there was so great a disturbance that the meeting came to an end. George, and several priests and professors, betook themselves to an inn in the neighbourhood, "where," says he, "I maintained the true Church, and the true Head of it, till they all gave out, and fled away."

The followers of George Fox appear to have been the first that applied the term "steeple-house" to a church. They regarded the building as a mere house, worthy of no more respect than ordinary houses; but, as it had a steeple, they called it a steeple-house for the sake of distinction.

He had not yet done with temptations. As he was sitting by the fire one morning, a great cloud seemed to come over him, and he appeared to hear a voice saying, "All things come by nature," when he felt himself under a temptation to believe that there was no God. He sat for a while in silence, deprived, as he fancied, of all power to think, till at last another voice rose within him, inspiring new hope, and saying, "There is a living God who made all things;" and the cloud that had darkened his mind then seemed to disperse. He wondered why he should have been troubled with such a temptation, but, after some days, he met with several people who affirmed that there was no God, and that all things came by nature. With these he had a long dispute, and at length, he says, overturned them, and then understood why he had been put through this mental exercise.

He now thought himself renewed in his mind, and imagined himself to be entering into a mental paradise. He fancied that the whole creation was opened to him, and that it was showed him how all things had their names given them according to their nature and virtue. The nature and properties of created things were so opened to him by Divine revelation, that he hesitated whether he ought not to practise physic for the good of mankind; but, after a while, it was intimated to him that his labour was to be spiritual. At the same time, his light gave him to see the three great deficiencies in the three great professions : that physicians knew nothing of the wisdom of God, by which the creatures were made, and therefore knew nothing of the virtues of the creatures ; that the priests were void of the true faith, and therefore could not please God ; and that the lawyers were destitute of genuine equity and justice, and therefore could not act conformably to the law of God, whose purity was grieved at the immorality of man. It was no wonder, consequently, that the world should be in so bad a condition, when the physicians, who had the charge of the body, the priests, who had the cure of souls, and the lawyers, who had the disposal of property, were all deficient in wisdom, and religion, and probity.. But God's light showed him also how all might be improved, and taught him that a total reformation might be effected if men would but listen to Divine admonitions, and not read the Scriptures without allowing them to make due impression on their minds; exclaiming against Cain, Balaam, and Judas, without considering that the dispositions of those offenders were still active in themselves.

He saw daily, with more and more clearness, that every man has some portion of Divine enlightenment; that those who attend to it, and foster it, come out of condemnation, and become the children of life; but that they who disregard it, and are heedless of its illumination, are condemned by it, whatever profession they may make. This he saw in the pure openings, as he calls them, of his own light, without help or instruction from any man; nor did he know then, he says, where to find authority for this belief in the Scriptures, though afterwards, in searching the Scriptures, he found it. Yet, at this time, he adds, " I had no slight esteem of the Holy Scriptures: they were indeed very precious to me; for I was in that Spirit by which they were given forth, and what the Lord opened in me, I afterwards found was agreeable to them." We thus see the conceit of the man, deeming the light that was in himself preferable to that which he could gain from the Scripture. He became more and more convinced that he was ordained to do great things; he dreamed that he was to go preaching through the world, which was like a briery and thorny wilderness; that priests and professors, magistrates and people, swelled and raged like the sea when he came with power among them; and that he was to be successful in turning many from darkness to light, and from error to truth, and in teaching mankind that the manifestation of the Spirit was given to every man and woman for their profit. He therefore proceeded in his course, to draw men from their earthly churches to the Divine Church; to lead them from worldly religion to the true religion, and from forms without power to sincere spiritual worship.

At this time, when he was still in the twenty-fourth year of his age, it was revealed to him by his inward light that he was not to take off his hat to any person, high or low; that he was to use, in addressing any single individual, of whatever rank, the pronouns *thou* and *thee;* that he was not to bid people good morrow or good evening; and that he was " not to bow or scrape with his leg to any one." His conduct in these respects put the priests and professors, and people of all sorts, into a great rage; " for," says he, " though *thou* to a single person was according to their own learning, their accidence and grammar rules, and according to the Bible, yet they could not bear to hear it, and the abstinence from the hat-honour set them all in a fury; but the Lord showed me that it was a worldly honour, which He would lay in the dust,—an honour which proud flesh looked for, while it forgot the honour from above. As Christ says, 'How can ye believe, who receive honour one of another?' But oh! the rage and scorn, the heat and fury, that arose! Oh! the blows, punchings, beatings, and imprisonments, that we underwent for not putting off our hats to men! For that soon tried all men's patience and sobriety what it was. Some had their hats violently plucked off, and thrown away, so that they quite lost them. The bad language and evil usage we received on this account is hard to be expressed, besides the danger we were in of sometimes losing our lives for this matter, and that by the great professors of Christianity, who thereby discovered that they were not true believers. But, blessed be the Lord! many came to see the vanity of that custom of putting off the hat to men, and felt the weight of truth's testimony against it."

The audacity of this young man, in thus setting himself up against the customs of the world, and obstinately refusing compliance with them, in spite of perpetual contumely and peril, is amazing.

But he felt himself irresistibly impelled to be a universal reformer. Every man, of every condition, was to listen to his warnings and admonitions. He proceeded to exhort judges and justices, orally and by letter, to do justly; to caution merchants and dealers against cheating and cozening; to testify against houses of entertainment where men got more than would do them good; to lift up his voice against wakes and feasts, May games, sports, plays, and shows, which led men to vanity and looseness of life, and desecrated days appointed to be kept holy; to protest against all kinds of music and all tricks of mountebanks on the stage; to charge the astrologers not to draw men's minds from the Sun of righteousness; to visit schoolmasters and mistresses, and counsel them to teach their children sobriety, and detestation of wantonness; and to call upon the masters and mistresses of families to train up their children and servants in the fear of God, and to make themselves examples of propriety and virtue to them. How all those upon whom he experimented received his advances, he does not tell us, but we may suppose that the more good-natured received him with kindness and pity, while the more surly would repel him with insult or ridicule.

But nothing offended him more than the sound of the bell which called people to the steeple-house; it grieved him to his inmost soul, for it seemed to him just like a market bell, to gather people together that the priest might set forth his wares to sale. He lamented the vast sums of money that are gotten by the trade which is made of selling the Scriptures, from the highest bishop to the lowest priest, notwithstanding that the Scriptures were given freely, that Christ commanded his ministers to preach freely, and that the prophets and apostles denounced judgment against all covetous hirelings and diviners for money.

As he was walking towards Nottingham on a Sunday morning, accompanied by some friends who were going to a meeting, his ears were struck by the bell of the great steeple-house, in sight of which he soon came, when his inward monitor told him that he must go yonder and cry against the great temple and the worshippers in it. He said nothing of this prompting to the friends that were with him, but attended them to the meeting, from which, as soon as he saw that the power of the Lord was properly manifested among them, he withdrew to the steeple-house, where he thought that the congregation looked like a wide piece of fallow ground, and the priest in his pulpit like a great clod of earth. The priest took for his text the words of Peter, " We have also a more sure word of prophecy," and told the people that it was by the Scriptures that they must try all religious doctrines and opinions.

" No," exclaimed George, excited by the mighty power within him, and unable to restrain himself from giving vent to his notions,—" no! it is not the Scriptures by which doctrines are to be tried, but the divine light by which the Scriptures were given; for the Jews had the Scriptures, and professed to try their doctrines by them, but erred in their judgment, and rejected Christ the Morning Star, because they formed their conclusions without attending to the divine light in their own minds."

As he was haranguing thus, interrupting the priest, and amazing the congregation, the constables very properly seized upon him, and carried him off to prison.

CHAPTER VI.

His condition in prison—His remarkable influence over the sheriff and his wife—He is released, and resumes his wanderings—He fancies that he works a miracle—He is almost killed by an enraged congregation—He is again ill-treated—He imagines that he works another miracle—His second imprisonment.

THE prison was pervaded by an offensive stench, with which George's nostrils were grievously annoyed. He had to endure it, however, till the evening, when they took him before the mayor, aldermen, and sheriffs of the town. The mayor happened to be in a peevish, fretful temper, "but," says George, "the power of the Lord allayed him." They questioned George, and George told them "that the Spirit had moved him

to go to the steeple-house that day to
address the people." This being the only
answer that they could get from him, they
sent him back to prison again. But some
time afterwards the head sheriff, whose
name was John Reckless, led George out of
prison, and brought him to his own house,
where his wife met George in the hall, took
him by the hand, and said, "Salvation is
come to our house;" for she, and her husband, and her whole family, were much affected and changed, according to George's
account, by the Divine power. George was
in consequence lodged in the sheriff's house,
where great meetings were held, and many
persons of good condition came to them.
The sheriff remembered that he and his
brother sheriff, who were partners in trade,
had wronged a woman in their dealings with
her, and sent for her, to her great surprise,
for she was not aware that she had been
wronged, and made restitution to her.   On

the next market-day the sheriff, as he was walking with George in the house, in his slippers, suddenly exclaimed, " I must go into the market and preach repentance to the people;" and he accordingly proceeded, not only into the market-place, but through several streets, in his slippers as he was, preaching to the people and exhorting them to repent. At this exhibition the magistrates were disgusted and incensed, and refused to connive any longer at George's residence in the sheriff's house, but remanded him to the common prison. Some one offered to take his place and suffer in his stead, but George did not consent. When the assizes came on, he was to have been brought before the judge, but the sheriff's men being tardy in fetching him, the judge had risen before he arrived, expressing his displeasure at having been made to wait, and saying that he would have admonished the youth if he had been placed before him.   As the youth, however, came too late to be admonished, he was sent back again to the gaol, where he suffered much annoyance from the rudeness of the inmates, until the governor of the castle put him under the protection of a body of soldiers.

He was kept prisoner, he says, "a pretty long time;" he does not specify how long, or how he came to be released.   But he was no sooner at liberty than he began to travel as before.   He came to Mansfield Woodhouse, where he gives us to understand that he wrought a miracle.   There was a distracted woman under the hands of a doctor, who was trying to bleed her, while people around were holding her down for the operation, but no blood could be extracted from her.   George told them to let her alone, as they could not touch the spirit in her by which she was tormented.   They accordingly let her go, and George was moved to speak to her, and to bid her, in the name of the Lord, be quiet and still. Quiet and still she became ; and the Lord's power settled her mind, and she mended ; and afterwards she received the truth, and continued in it to the day of her death.

"Many great and wonderful things," adds George, "were wrought by the heavenly power in those days; for the Lord made bare his omnipotent arm, and manifested his power to the astonishment of many, by the healing virtue whereof many have been delivered from great infirmities, and the devils were made subject through his name, of which particular instances might be given, beyond what this unbelieving age is able to receive or bear."

What the age was unable to bear, George discreetly forbears to relate.

The treatment which he had received in the steeple-house at Nottingham did not deter him from making another attempt to harangue the minister and the people in the steeple-house at Mansfield. But the congregation were not at all tolerant of his exhortation; they would not listen to him even for a moment, but rose upon him in great rage, beat him with their hands, bibles, and sticks, struck him down, and almost stifled and smothered him. They then dragged him forth, while he was scarcely able to stand, and put him in the stocks, where he was forced to sit some hours, while the people came about him with horsewhips, threatening to scourge him. At length they took him to the magistrate's, where a large number of the better class of people were assembled, who, thinking that he had been sufficiently punished, recommended that he should be set at liberty, being cautioned not to offend in a similar manner again. But the rabble were not so easily appeased, for they waylaid him as he went out, and stoned him till he was scarcely able to stand; nor was it without great difficulty that he escaped from the town; but, when he was about a mile from it, he met with people that gave him something to comfort him, which he greatly needed, being bruised, he says, inwardly as well as outwardly. "But the Lord's power," he adds, "soon healed me again."

He now thought proper to go from Nottinghamshire into Leicestershire, having a desire to confer with some Baptists, who had separated themselves from the Church. They met at Barrow. The conference was short, and unsatisfactory to the Baptists. When they spoke of their water-baptism, George Fox, and some friends who were with him, asked them who baptized John the Baptist. To this question they could make no answer, and George Fox and his party walked off in triumph.

After visiting some other places, he came to Market-Bosworth, on a Sunday when Nathaniel Stevens, the vicar of Drayton, where he was born, was about to preach. Seeing George addressing the people, he was greatly enraged, and told them that George was a madman, to whom they must by no means listen. The people were moved by what Stevens said, and, falling upon George and his companions, stoned them out of the town.

Some time afterwards he went to Twycross, and performed, as he intimates, another miracle. There was a great man in the place, who had long lain sick, and was given over by the physicians. Some of his friends requested George to see him. "I went up to him in his chamber," says George, "and spake the word of life to him, and was moved to pray by him; and the Lord was entreated, and restored him to health." But one of the man's servants, who doubted George's good intentions, waited for him as he came downstairs, and threatened to stab him with a naked rapier, which he held close to George's side. But George looked calmly at him, and said, "Alack for the poor creature! what wilt thou do with thy carnal weapon? It is no more to me than a straw." Those who stood by expressed their unwillingness that George should be stabbed; and so the man, repressed by their compassion and George's firmness, withdrew in a rage, and his master, as soon he heard of the affair, dismissed him from his service.

He was then moved to go into Derbyshire, and came first to Chesterfield, where he was taken before the mayor for interfering with a congregation, and sent ignominiously from the town by night. He next bent his course towards Derby, having two friends with him, and took a lodging at the house of a doctor, whose wife was of

George's way of thinking. On the following morning he was annoyed by hearing the bell of the steeple-house, and, on inquiring why it was rung, was told that there was to be a great lecture that day, at which many priests and officers of the army, and a colonel that was a great preacher, were to be present. George immediately felt himself moved to go to that congregation, and, when they had concluded the service, spoke to them what he felt prompted to say, and was heard without much opposition. But at last an officer came and took him by the hand, and told him that he and his two friends must go before the magistrates. The magistrates asked them why they had come to the church. George replied, that God had moved them to do so, and proceeded to exhort them not to think a steeple-house a church, or to trust in baptism. As they answered with some remonstrance, in which the name of Christ was introduced, George admonished them not to dispute of Christ, but to obey Him. The examination lasted from one o'clock in the afternoon till nine, George being several times sent out of the room. One of the questions that they asked him was, whether he was without sin. He replied yes, for Christ had taken away his sin. At last they committed George and one of his comrades, whose name was Fretwell, to the House of Correction for six months, as blasphemers.

CHAPTER VII.

FRETWELL proved but a false friend, and,
by gaining the keeper's favour, obtained
leave of the magistrates to go to see his
mother, and did not return. George, being
left alone, was often asked insidious questions by the keeper, to entrap him into
some foolish admissions, but George never
allowed him to effect his object.

During his confinement, being allowed
the use of pen and ink, he was moved
to write to the priests, magistrates, mayor,

and other people of Derby. The priests
he exhorted not to make a trade and
sale of what the apostles and prophets
had spoken; the magistrates he warned
not to fight against God; and the mayor
he requested to think on the parable of
Lazarus and Dives. It will be sufficient
to give one specimen of these epistles,
and I select that which he addressed to
the whole town of Derby:

"O Derby, as the waters run away
when the floodgates are up, so doth the
visitation of God's love pass away from
thee, O Derby! Therefore, look where
thou art, and how thou art grounded;
and consider, before thou art utterly forsaken. The Lord moved me twice before
I came to cry against the deceits and
vanities that are in thee, and to warn
all to look at the Lord, and not at man.
The woe is against the crown of pride,
and the woe is against drunkenness and

vain pleasures, and against them that make a profession of religion in words, and are high and lofty in mind, and live in oppression and envy. O Derby, thy profession and preaching stinks before the Lord. Ye do profess a Sabbath in words, and meet together, dressing yourselves in fine apparel, and you uphold pride. Thy women go with stretched-forth necks, and wanton eyes, &c., which the true prophet of old cried against. Your assemblies are odious, and an abomination to the Lord; pride is set up, and bowed down to; covetousness abounds; and he that doth wickedly is honoured; so deceit doth bear with deceit; and yet they profess Christ in words. O the deceit that is within thee! It doth even break my heart to see how God is dishonoured in thee, O Derby!"

It was well for George Fox's success in his enterprising course, that he was able to make more impression on those about him by his speech than he could have made by his writing. Croese represents him as not only unqualified to write legibly, but as unable to express his thoughts intelligibly on paper, and says that he was always obliged to employ others, who could put his meaning into significant words, to write for him. But Sewel affirms that this is at variance with truth; for though George was no elegant writer or good speller, yet his characters were tolerable, and his writing legible, and his matter, though not given in the style of a skilful linguist, was yet intelligible. "And albeit he employed others," he adds, "because himself was no quick writer, yet generally they were young lads, who, as they durst not have attempted to alter his words or phrases, so they would not have been skilful enough to refine his style. This I do not write from hearsay, but have seen it at sundry times." Croese is, however, very right in his observation that all Fox wrote in the epistolary way was little more than a rough collection, *rudis indigestaque moles*, of Scripture texts and phrases. As for his journal, he relates his fortunes in it in the rambling and tedious style of an illiterate visionary.

It was about the time of George's committal to the Derby House of Correction that he and his few followers began to be designated by the term Quakers. Gervas Bennett, one of the magistrates that committed him, was admonished by him to quake at the name of the Lord, when Bennett replied that George Fox and his followers might rather quake at the civil authorities,—a repartee which, going abroad among the multitude, occasioned Fox and his adherents to be called contemptuously Quakers. It cannot but be thought wonderful that a young man of five-and-twenty, of no learning, except in texts of Scripture, and little sound sense, should have been able to attract sufficient followers to form the foundation of a sect under any title.

After George had been in confinement a short time, the keeper of the House of Correction, who had been very violent against him at first, became more favourable towards him, in consequence of having had a dream of the day of judgment, in which he fancied he saw George Fox, and was afraid of him because he had done him so much wrong. So he went into George's apartment, and said, "I have been as a lion against you, but now I come like a lamb, and like the gaoler that came to Paul and Silas trembling, for I and my house have been plagued for your sake." He then entreated George to let him stay in the apartment, and confer with him, and George at last assented to his request. The particulars

E

of the conference we are not told, but the following morning the keeper went to the justices, and told them how he and his house had been plagued on George's account, when one of them, Justice Bennett, replied that plagues were on them too for keeping him. Soon afterwards the justices gave him liberty to walk out a mile whenever he pleased; but George declined to avail himself of the permission, saying that if they would mark out for him the exact length of a mile, he might take the liberty of walking it sometimes, but that, until they did so, he should keep himself within the house. George suspected that they made the proposal in the expectation that he would walk away altogether, and rid them of their plague; and he afterwards learned from the keeper that such was the case. Impatience of restraint, however, at last induced George to make use of the justices' permission, and he walked his mile, or what he conceived to be a mile, without insisting that it should be actually measured for him.

Sometimes, keeping within the mile, he would go into the market and the streets, and warn the people to repent of their wickedness. At other times he would employ himself in writing letters to be circulated among his friends and others, to enlighten or confirm them in the knowledge of what he thought the truth. In one of his general epistles, after exhorting his readers to mind the light and anointing that is within them, and bear the judgment of the world in patience, he observes, "The fleshly mind doth mind the flesh, and talketh fleshly, and its knowlege is fleshly, and not spiritual, but savours of death, and not of the spirit of life. Some men have the nature of swine, wallowing in the mire; some have the nature of dogs, to bite both the sheep of Christ and one another; some have the nature of lions, to tear, devour, and destroy; and some have the nature of the serpent (that old adversary), to sting, envenom, and poison. He that hath an ear to ear, let him hear, and learn these things within himself. And some men have the nature of other beasts and creatures, minding nothing but earthly and visible things, and feeding without the fear of God; some have the nature of a horse, to prance and vapour in their strength, and to be swift in doing evil; and some have the nature of tall, sturdy oaks, who are strong in evil, which must perish and come to the fire. Thus the evil is but one in all, but worketh many ways; and whatsoever a man's or woman's nature is addicted to, that is outward, the evil one will fit him with that, and will please his nature and appetite, to keep his mind in his inventions, and in the creatures from the Creator. Therefore, take heed of the enemy, and keep in the faith of Christ." This passage, from which we have omitted only a few superfluous words, is one of the best of George's effusions.

At length some of his relations, being concerned that he should be kept so long under restraint, made application to the justices for his discharge, offering to be bound in a hundred pounds, with others in fifty pounds each, that he should appear no more in Derby to preach against the priests; but George would not consent that they should be bound for him, as he had done, he said, no ill, but had merely spoken the word of life and truth to the people,—a declaration which so provoked Justice Bennett that he became George's enemy again; and, as George was kneeling down, before the bench, to pray that Justice Bennett might be forgiven, the justice ran upon him, and struck him with both his hands, and cried, "Away with him, gaoler!" George was accordingly remanded to the House of Correction till his six months should be expired.

At the conclusion of the term, the Parliament were raising soldiers, and the commissioners who were at Derby for that purpose, having heard of George's firmness and spirit, expressed a desire to make him a captain. He was accordingly brought before the commissioners in the market-place, where they offered him that distinction if he would consent to bear arms for the Commonwealth against Charles Stuart. But George replied that all wars arose from the lust of power and dominion, and that he had adopted, and wished others to adopt, such a mode of life as would take away all occasion for war. They thought that he did not really intend to decline the offer, and assured him that they made it in all love and kindness to him.

George retorted, with certainly very unnecessary warmth, that if that was their love and kindness, he trampled it under his feet. No one can be surprised that the commissioners should have been enraged, and that the magistrates should have ordered him back into confinement.

His confinement was now, however, less pleasant than before, for he was sent into the common dungeon, among a score and a half of felons, where he had no bed or convenience of any kind. Here, except that he was sometimes allowed to walk in the garden, he was kept for another six months, and a prophecy was circulated that he would never come out; but George was assured, by his inward light, that he should yet be delivered, and that God had still service for him to do.

His relations, and some of his other friends, came to see him again, and were much concerned that he should be thrust among felons for religion; but the way

in which he talked to them made many of
of them think that he was mad, and they
at last left him to himself.

He still continued to write letters to the
judges and others. One of the points on
which he admonished the judges, was, not
to put men to death for mere stealing, as
such severity was contrary to the law of
God and the Scriptures.

At last, the magistrates, in order to get
rid of him, determined on pressing him for
a soldier, seeing that he would not volun-
tarily enlist. They offered him press-money,
but he told them that he was bought off
from outward wars. He was then brought
before the commissioners, who attempted to
force him into the service; but he said
that he was dead to it. They replied that
he was alive, and offered him money twice,
but he still refused to take it, and incensed
the magistrates so much that they ordered
him to be kept close prisoner.

He still continued to tease them with

letters and admonitions, and they knew not
what to do with him; but, "at length,"
says George, "they were made to turn me
out of gaol, about the beginning of winter
in the year 1651, after I had been a prisoner
in Derby almost a year, six months in the
House of Correction, and the rest of the time
in the common gaol and dungeon."

CHAPTER VIII.

THE man Charles Stuart, against whom
the Parliamentary Commissioners wanted
George Fox to serve, was Charles II.; for
Charles I. had been beheaded on the 30th
of January, 1649, and his son, having
landed in Scotland in June, 1650, had, after
much unsatisfactory intercourse with the
Scots, and after having given his assent to
the covenant against Episcopacy, been received by them as King of Great Britain.

Cromwell had returned, from subduing Ireland, to put down the Scots, and had been opposed by Leslie, who, by cutting off supplies for his army, and other means, had gained some advantage over him, and, but for the folly of the Presbyterian preachers, would probably have driven him ignominiously from the country. He had been obliged to retire towards Dunbar, where Leslie had got possession of the heights and passes, and had reduced Cromwell to fear that he must either be starved, or must send off a portion of his force to England by sea, and attempt to cut his way through the enemy with the rest; but the fanaticism of the Scottish ecclesiastics, who declared that they saw visions of victory, had such influence with the army, a body under no proper control, that Leslie was forced to leave his excellent position, and risk a battle with Cromwell on his own ground. The ill-disciplined Scots, though double the

number of the English, were little qualified to cope with Cromwell's veterans, and
yielded him a complete victory, on the 3rd of
September, 1650.

A Scottish force, however, was still
kept together, and Charles was crowned
at Scone on the 1st of January, 1651.
Cromwell had left the way southward open,
and Charles, in the following summer, had
influence enough with a body of the Scots,
amounting to about twelve thousand, to
march with him into England.   They
reached Worcester, but, before they could
receive any great accession of strength,
were overtaken by Cromwell, who gave
them a total defeat on the 3rd of September, 1651.   Charles, after many well-
known adventures and perils, effected his
escape to Normandy.

It was in this state of things, when
Cromwell was bent upon securing absolute
power, that George Fox was let loose from

Derby gaol. He proceeded as before in what he thought the work of the Lord, and went about teaching and exhorting, first into his own county of Leicester, and afterwards into Staffordshire. Here he was guilty of one of the most extravagant manifestations of folly that he ever exhibited. I shall relate it exactly as he relates it himself in his own journal. Were it told by any one else, we should of necessity suppose that there must be some exaggeration in the account. As he was walking along, he says, with several friends, he lifted up his head, and saw three steeple-house spires, which, as he expresses it, struck at his life. He asked his companions what place that was, and they told him Lichfield; and immediately the word of the Lord came to him that he must go thither. He said nothing to his friends, however, of his intention to do so, but went with them to a house where they were to stop, and, as soon as he saw them fairly lodged, stole away from them, and scampered in a straight line over hedges and ditches till he came to a field within a mile of Lichfield, where there were some shepherds keeping sheep. "There," says he, "I was commanded by the Lord to pull off my shoes; and I stood still, for it was winter, and the word of the Lord was like a fire in me. So I put off my shoes, and left them with the shepherds, and the poor shepherds trembled and were astonished. Then I walked on about a mile till I came into the city, and as soon as I got within the city, the word of the Lord came to me again, saying, 'Cry, Woe unto the bloody city of Lichfield!' So I went up and down the streets, crying with a loud voice, 'Woe to the bloody city of Lichfield!' And, it being market-day, I went into the market-place, and to and fro in the several parts of it, and made stands, crying as before, 'Woe to the bloody city of Lichfield!' And no one laid hands on me; but as I went thus crying through the streets, there seemed to me to be a channel of blood running down the streets, and the market-place appeared like a pool of blood. Now when I had declared what was upon me, and felt myself clear, I went out of the town in peace, and, returning to the shepherds, gave them some money, and took my shoes of them again. But the fire of the Lord was so in my feet, and all over me, that I did not matter to put on my shoes any more, and was at a stand whether I should or no till I felt freedom from the Lord so to do; and then, after I had washed my feet, I put on my shoes again. After this a deep consideration came upon me," says he, as indeed might well be the case, "why, or for what reason, I should be called to cry against that city, and call it the bloody city. For though the Parliament had the minster one while and the king another while, and much blood had been shed in the town during the wars between them, yet that was no more than had befallen many other places. But afterwards I came to understand that in the Emperor Diocletian's time a thousand Christians were martyred in Lichfield. So I was to go, without my shoes, through the channel of their blood, and into the pool of their blood in the market-place, that I might raise up the memorial of the blood of those martyrs which had been shed above a thousand years before, and lay cold in their streets. So the sense of this blood was upon me, and I obeyed the word of the Lord. Ancient records testify how many of the Britons suffered there; and much I could write of the sense I had of the blood of the martyrs that had been shed in this nation for the name of

Christ, both under the ten persecutions and since; but I leave it to the Lord, and to His book, out of which all shall be judged."

After this display, his relations, who thought him mad when he was in Derby gaol, may be considered to have had some reason for their opinion. What astonishes us in the present day, is, that, after such an egregious indication of insanity, he should still have found people to think him worthy to be their leader. He is doubtless guilty of anachronism in his account, for he must be supposed to have heard of the martyrdom at Lichfield, which is a common story, before he started on his course over hedge and ditch to bawl the words of Ezekiel in the streets without his shoes. Why people who lived a thousand years after the martyrdom were to be reviled or punished for the deeds of those from whom they were not perhaps even descended, George's light seems to have left him quite uninformed; nor does it appear that the town of Lichfield was at all affected by his denunciations, since it was in the same condition after his vagary as before; so that he was commanded to take off his shoes, and to fancy his bare feet trampling in blood, to no purpose. To this adventure of George's, Sewel, who gives a long account of him, and transcribes largely from his journal, takes care not even to allude. Croese, who is less partial, gives it at full length.

George then travelled through parts of Nottinghamshire and Derbyshire, and passed into Yorkshire, and went, he says, to Captain Parsloe's house in Selby, who was friendly to him. This is the first time that he mentions Captain Parsloe, and it does not appear, from anything that he says of him; what sort of captain he was. "I had a horse," adds George Fox, "but was fain to leave him, for I was moved to go to many great houses, to admonish and exhort people to turn to the Lord." The horse, we might have supposed, would have been of some service in conveying him to the many great houses, but George, it seems, thought otherwise. Having left his horse, he was moved to go to Beverley steeple-house; he arrived in Beverley on a Saturday evening, drenched with rain, and, having slept at an inn, got up in the morning, paid what was due, and proceeded, with his clothes still wet, to the steeple-house, where the preacher was delivering his sermon. When he had concluded, George was moved to speak to him and to the congregation; and his words were so strong, he says, that they struck a mighty dread among the people. The mayor came forward and spoke to him, but none of them had any power to meddle with him. In the afternoon he went to another steeple-house, and addressed the priest and the people in a similar manner; the priest said to him, "I am but a child, and cannot dispute with you." The priests in both places probably thought George a harmless fanatic, about whom it was not worth while to make any disturbance.

George went back to Captain Parsloe's, and the captain attended him to Justice Hotham's, who was willing to listen to George. While he was at the justice's, a great woman came to see him about some business, and happened to observe to him, that on the preceding Sunday an angel or spirit had come into the church at Beverley, and had spoken wonderful things, astonishing priest, magistrates, and people, and that, when it ceased to speak, it passed away, leaving no indication whence it came or whither it went. This Justice Hotham mentioned to George, who was mightily pleased that he and his leather suit should have been taken for an angel.

He continued during the week with Captain Parsloe and Justice Hotham, and on the following Sunday went to another steeple-house, where the priest took for his text, "Ho, every one that thirsteth, come ye to the waters, and he that hath no money, come ye, buy, and eat; yea, come, buy wine and milk, without money and without price." As he was leaving the pulpit, George was moved to say to him, "Come down, thou deceiver; dost thou bid people come freely, and yet thou takest three hundred pounds a year of them, for preaching the Scriptures to them? Mayest thou not blush for shame? Did the prophet Isaiah, and Christ, do so, who spake the words, and gave them forth freely? Did not Christ say to his ministers, whom He sent to preach, 'Freely ye have received, freely give'?" The priest, he says, hastened away like a man amazed, and left George ample time to address the people, whom he endeavoured to lead into the right path.　When he returned to Justice Hotham's house, the justice took him in his arms, and said that his house was George's house, so exceedingly glad was he that the divine power was thus revealed.

Quitting the justice and the captain, he came to an inn, where there was a company of rude people, and told the woman of the house, if she had any meat, to bring him some; but, as he said "thee" and "thou" to her, she testified no willingness to accommodate him.　He then asked her if she had any milk or cream, and she replied in the negative; but there was a churn in the room, and a child playing near it, who happened to put his hand on it and overturn it, when the cream was all scattered over the floor before the woman's face; this George considered to be a judgment on the woman for her falsehood and perverseness. But George was not at all benefited by it, for he was obliged to leave the house and walk on until he found a haystack, at the side of which he passed the night amidst rain and snow, the time being about three days before Christmas.

In this plight he went the next day to York, and was moved to visit the cathedral, where, after the service was concluded, he proceeded to admonish the people; but the people were not so tolerant as they had been in some other places, for they told him it was too cold to stay listening to him, and, hurrying him out, threw him down the steps.

From York he went to Cleaveland, and from thence to a village called Stath. Here he had a dispute with the leader of some Ranters, at which two priests were present, one a Scotchman, and the other named Philip Scafe, who was inclined to George's way of thinking. George stopped the mouth of the Ranter, and, after the meeting was over, the Scotch priest asked George to walk with him to the top of the cliffs, and discuss some points of doctrine with him. George consented, provided that a brother-in-law of the priest should accompany them as a witness, lest anything should be reported of George which he did not say. George replied to such questions as the Scotch priest put to him, and they parted without any signs of animosity ; but, as the priest was going away, he met Philip Scafe, to whom he expressed himself with the greatest bitterness against George, and said, that, if ever he met him again, he would have George Fox's life, or George Fox should have his. George's friends, in consequence, thought that the priest had invited George to walk with him alone with the intention of pushing him over the cliff, and putting an end to him, but that his design was frustrated by the presence of a third person. "After some years, however," says George, "this very Scotch priest, and his wife also, came to be convinced of the truth and about twelve years after I was at their house."

In other places in that part of the country, where George had disputes with the priests, and offered exhortations to the people, he says that the Divine word in his mouth was so powerful that it "reached to the hearts of people, and made both priests and professors tremble. It shook the earthly and airy spirit in which they held their profession of religion and worship, so that it was a dreadful thing unto them when it was told them, 'The man in leathern breeches is come!' At the hearing thereof, the priests in many places would get out of the way; they were so struck with the dread of the eternal power of God, and fear surprised the hypocrites."

He was now making some impression on one or two, here and there, of the better class of people; and at Pickering, one Justice Robinson, and an old priest of his acquaintance, showed him great favour, the justice highly commending George for exercising the gift that God had given him.

The priest accompanied him to a village in the neighbourhood, where there was held a great meeting, to which professors of several sorts came. George took his post on a haystack, where he sat silent for some hours, "for," says he, "I was to famish them from words." The people grew impatient, and asked the priest, from time to time, when George would begin. The priest told them to wait calmly, as the people sometimes waited a long while for Christ before He spoke. At last George was moved to speak, and the audience were struck with the power of the word of life, and there was "a general convincement," he says, "among them."

He returned, after a while, to Justice

Hotham and Captain Parsloe, who were delighted to hear of the favour shown him by Justice Robinson, and observed that unless the principle of light and life, which was preached by George Fox, had been raised up and spread abroad, the nation would have been overrun with Ranterism.

How George lived during his wanderings, is a point that has greatly perplexed the readers of his journal. A man of such poor parentage could have little or no means of his own; he makes no mention of money being given him by others, and he maintained that those who preached the Gospel were to preach it without hire or recompence. Yet he seems always to have had money, more or less, at his command, and we find him, as he proceeds, in possession of a horse, and apparelled not in a suit of leather, but in the dress of a decent member of society. Croese gives the following account of the mode in which he subsisted:—"The ministers of the Church," he said, "were induced only by love of reward or hire to preach the Gospel, which should be preached gratuitously to all men; but he never considered how near akin his own case was to theirs; for, though he pretended to take all this pains and trouble in travelling about to preach the Gospel without reward, yet those to whom he preached supplied his necessities before he asked of them: at least he was never denied the liberty of coming uncalled for, as the flies, and of feeding, like the mice, on others' provision." Sewel and Gough are silent upon this subject, but it must have been by aid, of whatever kind, from his adherents, that George was enabled to sustain himself.

CHAPTER IX.

AFTER some further wandering, he reached a village named Patrington, where he happened to meet the clergyman in the street, and began to exhort him, and such of his flock as were at hand, to repent and turn to the right way. A multitude soon gathered round, but few listened with patience; and when he had concluded, and sought lodging at an inn, he was refused all accommodation. He

begged for a little meat or milk, offering
to pay them for it, but they would not
let him have it. He then went out of
the village, followed by a number of fellows jeering him, and sought something
to eat at the houses, but was everywhere
refused; so that, when it grew dark, he
was driven to get water from a ditch,
and to take shelter among some furze till
break of day. When he reappeared in
the morning, he was again seized by the
mob, and taken back to Patrington, whence,
after having been supplied by a villager,
somewhat more tender-hearted than his fellows, with a little milk and bread to keep
him from starving, he was conveyed nine
miles to a justice, whose custom was to
get drunk early in the day. When George
was brought before him, and kept his
hat on, and addressed him with the pro-
noun "thou," he asked the people around
whether the prisoner was not mad or

foolish; but George told him that he was acting according to his principles, and exhorted him to repent and come to the light with which Christ had enlightened every man. To the astonishment of all that were present, the justice, instead of ridiculing George, said very quietly, "Ay, you mean the light that is mentioned in the third of John." He then took George into a little parlour, and desired to see what letters or papers he had about him; George showed him that he had no letters, and, as he opened his leather suit, exhibited such clean linen as convinced the justice that he could not be a common vagrant; and he was accordingly set at liberty. A man who had witnessed the proceedings, took him to his house, and desired him to go to bed, or lie down on the bed, that he might say that he had seen him in or on a bed, for people had spread a report that George would not lie on any bed; a report to which his frequent necessity of lying out of doors had given rise.

Other strange reports were circulated respecting him, by persons who wished to exasperate the public against him. It was said that he carried a bottle of liquor about him, of which he made people drink to oblige them to follow him; and that he often rode a great black horse, on which he was seen at two places, sixty miles distant, at the same time.

Continuing his travels, he came to Gainsborough, where a great tumult arose about him, in consequence of an accusation brought against him of having said that he was Christ; but George assured the people that he had made no such assertion, but had merely said that it was Christ who spoke in him. At Warnsworth he was stoned by the rabble, and at Doncaster he experienced similar treatment, and was carried before the magistrates, who threatened that, if ever he came thither again, they would leave him to the mercy of the mob. At Tickhill he was beaten by the clerk with a heavy Bible, till the blood gushed from his nostrils, and afterwards dragged out of the place by the multitude, and thrown over a hedge, losing, at the same time, his hat, which he never recovered, and without which he had to travel to Balby, seven or eight miles off.

Notwithstanding all this contumely and discouragement, he still persevered in his course, and his doctrines began to be spread by others as well as himself. Some of his followers started forth to preach publicly; the first of whom were Thomas Aldam, Richard Farnsworth, William Dewsbury, John Audland, Edward Burrough, and Francis Howgill. The first four of these were humble and illiterate men; the other two had some education. Howgill had been at some university, and had then become a preacher among the Independents. Burrough was of a respectable family in Westmoreland, and had followed the Presbyterians for a time, but had deserted them on hearing George Fox, whom he seems somewhat to have resembled in character, haranguing a multitude.

With Richard Farnsworth and some others, he travelled about to various places. One day they came to a house at Bradford, and the people of the house set meat before them; but just as George was going to eat, the word of the Lord came to him, saying, "Eat not the bread of such as have an evil eye;" so he immediately arose from the table and ate nothing, the woman of the house being, as he afterwards discovered, a Baptist.

"As we travelled on," he says on another

occasion, "we came near a very great and high hill, called Pendle Hill, and I was moved of the Lord to go up to the top of it, which I did with much ado, it was so very steep and high. When I was come to the top of this hill, I saw the sea bordering upon Lancashire; and from the top of this hill, the Lord let me see in what places He had a great people to be gathered. As I went down, I found a spring of water in the side of the hill, with which I refreshed myself, having eaten or drunk but little in several days before."

The night following he was shown, in a vision, a great people in white raiment by a river-side, coming to the Lord, the scene of the vision being about Wentzerdale and Sedbergh. But while he had dreams of comfort to others, he enjoyed little comfort himself, for he lay that night upon a bed of fern, on an open common.

Going into Lancashire, and attempting to address a congregation at Newton-Cartmell, he was thrown headlong over a stone wall. But, at Ulverston, he was received with civility at Justice Fell's, in whose house he had much disputation with the clergyman of the parish, named Lampitt, to the great edification of the justice and his wife Margaret, who were enabled to see through the priest. There being a fast-day soon after, Margaret Fell asked George to go to the steeple-house, but George replied that he could only do as he should be directed by the Lord. He therefore walked out into the fields, and there the word of the Lord came to him, saying, "Go to the steeple-house after them." When he arrived at the steeple-house, the priest Lampitt was singing with his people, apparently at the conclusion of the service, but George thought the priest's spirit so foul, and the matter that he sang so unsuitable to the minds of his hearers, that, when they had done singing, he was moved to speak to him and to his congregation. He held forth on his usual topics. Justice Sawrey, one of the audience, desired the constables to take him away; but Margaret Fell requested that he might be allowed to speak, and the priest, probably to please Margaret Fell, seconded the request. He was therefore permitted to proceed for a time, but Justice Sawrey at length grew tired, and had him expelled from the church, to finish his sermon in the churchyard. Afterwards Justice Sawrey became more favourable to George, having heard much commendation of him from Justice Robinson, of Pickering, who had praised him for exercising his gifts.

Some priests having met at Justice Fell's house, George asked them whether any one of them could say that he had ever received a divine command to go and speak to any particular people. Some answered one thing and some another, and most of them would give no direct answer to the question; but, at last, one of them confessed that he had never heard any divine voice to send him to any people, but had merely preached as others did. This confession, says George, strengthened Justice Fell's inclination to believe that the priests were wrong, "for he had thought formerly, as the generality of people did, that they were sent from God."

In a while, Justice Sawrey's disposition towards George seems to have changed, for when, after some peregrinations, he returned to Ulverston again, and proceeded, as before, to address the congregation in Mr. Lampitt's church, Justice Sawrey came up to him, and charged him to speak according to the Scriptures. George looked astonished that he should thus address him, and replied that he would speak according to the Scriptures, and bring the Scriptures to prove what he had to say. But there seems to have been something in George's reply that offended the justice, for he soon refused to allow

George to speak any longer, and stirred up the rabble to beat and ill-use him. The people, in consequence, fell upon George in the church, before the justice's face, knocked him down, kicked him, and trampled on him, till, at last, the justice took him from among them, led him out of the church, consigned him to the constables, and bade them whip him and put him out of the town. The constables and others, accordingly, dragged him by the shoulders about a quarter of a mile out of the place; but some took George's part, and there was much contention, and several broken heads, and Justice Fell's son, who followed to watch the proceedings, was thrown into a ditch. At last, the party adverse to George prevailed, and, getting some hedge-stakes and holly-branches, dressed him till he fell senseless. When he recovered a little, he found himself lying on a wet common, and the people standing about him, and

after he had lain quiet a while, he says,
"the power of the Lord sprang through
him, and the eternal refreshings refreshed
him," so that he stood up invigorated, and,
stretching out his arms among the multitude, cried, "Strike again! here are my
arms, my head, and my cheeks."   A mason
took him at his word, and, aiming a blow at
him with his staff, struck him violently on
the back of the hand, so that his arm was
for a while benumbed, and the people thought
that he would never have the use of it
again; but in a few moments the divine
power sprang through him once more, and
he recovered strength in his hand and arm,
in the sight of them all.   Then, being
moved with love towards his persecutors,
he declared to them the word of life in return for their evil treatment, and they, probably thinking that they had gone far enough,
listened to him.   When he came to examine
his person in the evening, he found that his

body and arms were yellow, black, and blue, with the blows that he had received. Justice Fell was from home at the time that this violence took place.

At Walney Island, which is not far distant from Ulverston, George received even worse treatment; for a woman named Lancaster stirred up her neighbours against him, in the persuasion that he had bewitched her husband, and about forty people set upon him, with staves, clubs, and fishing-poles, crying, "Kill him! kill him!" so that he narrowly escaped with life. Margaret Fell, hearing of his disaster, sent a horse to bring him off; but, it was long before he was able to ride without great pain.

About this time, Justices Sawrey and Thompson granted a warrant against George, on an accusation that he had uttered blasphemy. He was, in consequence, obliged to appear at Lancaster, whither Justice Fell accompanied him; and a priest and two priests' sons charged him with having said that God taught deceit, and that the Scripture contained lies. There seemed, however, to be little ground for the charge, and George Fox was allowed to speak for himself, like Paul before Felix; when he said, "that his words, on the occasion to which they alluded, had been, that the Scriptures were given forth by the Spirit of God, and that the same Spirit must be in those who would understand the Scriptures." Upon this a priest, named Jackus, cried out "that the spirit and the letter were inseparable." "Then," retorted George, "every one that hath the letter hath the spirit, and the spirit of the Scripture may be bought with the letter." "Yes," added Justice Fell and Colonel West, a magistrate favourable to George, "people may carry the spirit of the Scripture in their pockets, as they carry the volume." The affair ended in the discharge of George; and Justices Sawrey and Thompson were afterwards less inclined to grant warrants against the Quakers, being persuaded by Justice Fell and Colonel West, that such warrants rather tended to encourage riots than peace.

CHAPTER X.

Increase of George's preachers—Account of Solomon Eccles—George's letters to the priest and people of Ulverston.

THE number of George's assistant preachers, better and worse, is said to have now amounted to twenty-five. Most of them appear to have been treated by mobs, here and there, in much the same way as their pertinacious leader; and very few of them seem to have been deterred by the buffetings and stonings that they incurred from prosecuting the object to which they had devoted themselves. All were ready to refuse "hat-homage" to men in authority; to "thee" and "thou" every one; to impress upon the people that steeple-houses were not more sacred than other houses; and to defy opposition and malice by endurance of duckings and scourgings, and by submitting to lie under haystacks at night in the open air.

One of the most extraordinary of his followers was the notorious Solomon Eccles, whose egregious extravagancies require more than a slight notice. We find a tolerably full account of him in Croese. He was a man, says that historian, void, not of understanding, but of all shame and fear, who was guilty of such monstrous outrages as it is wonderful that the Quakers should have been willing to record; showing, however, that there is nothing so absurd and offensive which some will not be ready to commit, if they may thus inflict insult or vengeance on those who have opposed or annoyed them. Eccles was originally a musician, having learned his art from his father, and possessed of such skill that he could

maintain a family in plenty, being able
to gain by teaching not less than two
hundred pounds a year. But he was
seized with a desire to change his mode
of life, and to join the society of the
Quakers. He accordingly proceeded to
sell his music books and instruments, as
being useless or noxious to him, and
obtained a considerable sum for them;
but, afterwards reflecting that they might
be hurtful to those who had bought them,
and that he ought not to suffer others
to be injured for his profit, he purchased
them back again for the money which
he had received, and then, having collected them together, carried them to
Tower Hill, where he laid them on a
pile of wood, and set fire to them at
noon-day, in the sight of numbers of
people, whom he exhorted to follow his
example, by shunning all empty and profane pursuits, and destroying whatever

they possessed that would lead them into vanity and folly. But he was not satisfied with going over to a new form of religion; he felt also an impulse to deride the established worship of the kingdom.

When he had ceased to be a musician, he became a shoemaker, and one Sunday morning, when the congregation were assembled in Aldermanbury Church, and the sacrament was to be administered, he went into the church with a bag of tools and some leather, intending to show his contempt for a steeple-house by working at his trade in it before the people. While they were singing a psalm, before the preacher went into the pulpit, he rushed up with his hat on into the chancel, with a view to get into the pulpit himself and ply his awl in it. But being obstructed by the people who stood round, he next made an effort to jump upon the communion-table. Being impeded, however, in this attempt also, he remained standing and looking about him, when some of the people, after the psalm was ended, took his hat off his head, and put it into his hand; he put it on again; but at last the clerk came forward, and, with the assistance of some of the by-standers, succeeded in getting him out at the door.

But, conceiving himself moved by the Spirit to make another attempt, he returned on the following Sunday, equipped with his implements as before, to the same church, and, while the preacher was in the vestry preparing for the sermon, rushed forward, in a frenzy of zeal, over the seats and heads of the people, into the pulpit, where he immediately pulled out his shoemaker's tools, and began to sew. A strong fellow pulled him down, and he struggled to get up again, but was at last forced out of the church and carried on the following day, amidst the hootings and insults of the mob, before the Lord Mayor, who put him into prison.

How long he was kept in confinement we are not told; but, when he got free, he became a preacher, and published a challenge, in imitation of Elijah's defiance to the priests of Baal, inviting Presbyterians, Independents, Baptists, and all of whatever sect or persuasion, to try by experiment with him who were the true worshippers of God; proposing that they should devote themselves for seven days and nights, without either meat or drink, to prayer and psalm-singing, and that those on whom celestial fire should first descend should be considered to have received the Divine approbation. But as none were found foolish enough to accept this challenge, he went into Scotland, and, hearing of a meeting of papists that was to take place in Galloway, went among them, attended by three of his associates, with a chafing dish of fire and brimstone on his head, denouncing that they should all be devoured with flames if they did not instantly forsake their idolatry. Escaping from hence, and commencing a similar admonition to the people of Edinburgh, he was beaten and thrown into gaol. On his enlargement, he returned to London, where he made a similar exhibition in Bartholomew Fair, and was almost torn to pieces by the multitude. He then went to Ireland, and, entering the great church at Cork during the time of service, he thundered out, " The prayers of the wicked are an abomination to the Lord;" for which outrage he was whipped through the streets by the hangman. His chafing dish and cry of " Woe, woe," afterwards excited the wonder of the Londoners during the plague.

Yet with this senseless fanatic, George Fox formed an intimate connection, and took him with him in his travels.

As for George, he stayed some days at Lancaster after he was discharged, and some of the lower class of people formed a plot to entice him out of his dwelling, and throw him over Lancaster Bridge; but their devices did not succeed. They then conceived another scheme; they brought to one of his meetings a distracted man, carrying bundles of rods, with which they designed to make him whip George; but George was moved to speak to them by the Divine power, which chained down the distracted man and all the others: he then bade the man throw his rods into the fire, and he obeyed the command, and they all departed in quiet.

Soon afterwards he wrote letters to the people of Ulverston, its priest, and its congregation. The letter to the priest began, "The word of the Lord to thee, O Lampitt;" that to the congregation, "The word of the Lord to all the people that follow priest Lampitt, who is a blind guide." They are all in George's ordinary rambling style. In the epistle to the congregation, turning from the people to the pastor, he says, "Thou, O Lampitt, deceivest the people, and feedest them with thy fancies, and makest a trade of the Scriptures, and takest them for thy cloak. But thou art manifest to all the children of light; for that cloak will not cover thee, but thy skirts are seen, and thy nakedness appears. And the Lord made one to go naked among you, a figure of thy nakedness, and of your nakedness, and as a sign amongst you, before your destruction cometh, that you might see that you were naked, and not covered with the truth." Who it was that thus exhibited himself or herself among priest Lampitt's congregation, or when the exhibition took place, George does not tell us; nor do we learn from any other quarter. Hume tells us of a similar appearance of a female Quaker in a church, who told the people that she was commanded to be a sign unto them.

CHAPTER XI.

George believes himself a prophet, a worker of miracles, and a discerner of spirits—He finds no favour at Carlisle, but is imprisoned, and terribly illtreated by the gaoler—He is released through an application to Cromwell's Parliament—Dissemination of Quakerism.

ABOUT this time, being now in the twentyninth year of his age, George relates that he had "great openings," not only of divine and spiritual matters, but also of outward things relating to the civil government. For, being one day at Swarthmore, when Justice Fell and Justice Benson were talking of the Parliament then sitting, called the Long Parliament, he was moved to tell them that before that day two weeks the Parliament would be broken up, and the speaker plucked out of his chair; a prediction which was fulfilled, for Oliver Cromwell had broken up the Parliament by that time.

Soon after, he was " in a fast for about ten days," his spirit being greatly exercised on truth's behalf, partly with reference to one Richard Myer, who had gone into great pride and exaltation of spirit; and George, going to a meeting at Arnside, where Richard Myer, who had been long lame of one of his arms, was, he was moved to say to him, in the midst of the people, " Prophet Myer, stand up upon thy legs! " when Myer stood up, and stretched out his lame arm, and said, " Be it known to you, all people, that this day I am healed! " Myer's parents could hardly believe it, but, on taking off his doublet, they saw it was true. But, after this, the Lord commanded him to go to York with a message, and he was disobedient; and the Lord, says George, struck him again, so that he died about three-quarters of a year after.

Being at a village in the same neighbourhood, declaring the word of life, he chanced to cast his eye upon a woman in whom he discerned an unclean spirit; and he was moved to speak sharply to her, and to tell her that she was a witch. The woman, of whom he had known nothing previously, left the room, and the people wondered, and told him afterwards that he had discovered a great thing, for all the county looked upon her to be a witch. "The Lord," says he, "had given me a spirit of discerning, by which I many times saw the states and conditions of people, and could try their spirits; for not long before, as I was going to a meeting, I saw some women in a field, and I discerned them to be witches, and I was moved to go out of my way into the field to them, and declare unto them their conditions, telling them plainly they were in the spirit of witchcraft. At another time there came such a one into Swarthmore Hall, in the meeting time, and I was moved to speak sharply to her, and told her she was a witch; and the people said afterwards she was generally accounted so."

At another meeting he set his eyes upon one of the Baptist deacons, who was crying out in a rage against George and his party, and the deacon, feeling George's power, exclaimed, "Do not pierce me so with thine eyes; keep thy eyes off me."

At one place he harangued a multitude, consisting of several hundreds, for three hours. At another he told his audience "that there had been a night of apostasy since the apostles' days, but that now the everlasting Gospel was preached again."

Thus he went on in his imaginations till he thought fit to visit Carlisle, where the magistrates did not approve of the harangues that he delivered and the crowds

that he collected, and thought it better
to stop his progress. He was accordingly
brought before them, and, after a long examination, committed to prison as a blas-
phemer, heretic, and seducer. He was put
into a tolerable room, and kept till the
assizes came on, when the high sheriff,
whose name was Wilfrey Lawson, was
anxious, if possible, to have him hanged.
But on consulting with the magistrates how
his death might be effected, he found that
he could not well be put upon his trial for
anything that he had said or done. Antony
Pearson, a justice of the county, who had become a follower of Fox, wrote to the judges
to entreat that he might be brought before
them, trusting that he would be discharged;
but the judges, who seem to have thought
that Fox had better be put down, declined
to take cognizance of him, and left him to
the mercy of the magistrates. In consequence, after the judges were gone, his place

of confinement was changed, and he was put into the common dungeon among thieves and other malefactors, and ill-treated, in various ways, both by the gaoler and under-gaoler. The under-gaoler would beat off any of Fox's friends that came to speak with him at the grate, with a cudgel, and one day he fell with his cudgel upon Fox himself, on pretence of driving him from the grate; but "while he struck me," says Fox, "I was made to sing in the Lord's power, and that made him rage the more. Then he went and fetched a fiddler, and brought him in where I was, and set him to play, thinking to vex me thereby; but while he played, I was moved in the ever-lasting power of the Lord God to sing, and my voice drowned the noise of the fiddle, and struck and confounded them, and made them give over fiddling and go their ways."

Whilst he was here, Justice Benson's wife was moved of the Lord to come to visit him, and to eat no meat but what she ate with him at the bars of the dungeon window. Justices Benson and Pearson, who applied for leave to visit him in prison, were not permitted; and they, in consequence, addressed a remonstrance to the magistrates, similar in character to George's own effusions, in which they admonished them that the Lord was coming to thrash the mountains and beat them to dust, and to take vengeance on all corrupt rulers and officers.

But a more efficient address was sent at the same time to the New Parliament, which had been recently summoned by Cromwell, stating that a person was confined in Carlisle gaol who was likely to die for religion. The Parliament despatched a letter on the subject to the sheriff and the other magistrates, who shortly after set George Fox at liberty.

George then proceeded through various

parts of the North of England, and was more followed after his imprisonment, perhaps in consequence of it, than before. He and his twenty-five or more preachers increased the number of Quakers wonderfully. It now began to be said that they would eat up one another : for many of them, after meetings, to which they came from a great distance, lodged at their friends' houses, often in greater numbers than there were beds to accommodate; and it was predicted that this hospitality would cause poverty, and that, when the Quakers had devoured one another's provisions, they would fall chargeable on the parishes. But the contrary proved to be the case, for many of the Quakers prospered greatly. At first, when they refused to take off their hats to their customers, and neglected other ways of the world, they lost much of their trade, as others were shy of dealing with them, so that many of them could scarcely for a time get money to buy bread. But after a while, when people came to understand their general honesty and faithfulness,—virtues to which they appear, in their earlier days, to have rigidly adhered,—many of them had more business than their neighbours; and the envious began to cry out that, if the Quakers were let alone, they would draw the whole trade of the nation into their hands. This became a fresh reason for persecuting them.

CHAPTER XII.

THE Parliament which Cromwell had assembled after the dissolution of the Long Parliament, had now resigned its power into Cromwell's hands, who had in consequence become sole ruler of the kingdom, assuming the title of Lord Protector.

On investing himself with the supreme authority, he required that the soldiers should take the oath of fidelity to him; but

Quakerism had now begun to appear in the army, and some of those who had become affected with it declared that they were forbidden by their principles to swear. These objectors appear to have been discharged. Among them Sewel mentions John Stubbs, who, he says, was skilled in Latin, Greek, Hebrew, and the Oriental languages, and, having become a thorough convert to George Fox's doctrines, was subsequently an eminent preacher among the Quaker community, and travelled, to make proselytes, over various parts of Europe, and to Egypt and America.

Meetings began to be held about this time in London. The first that presided at them were Francis Howgill and Antony Pearson, the justice that took the part of George Fox at Carlisle. At these assemblies women began to speak.

Francis Howgill seems to have been the first that made application to Cromwell for favour

to the Quakers.   He and some others appear
to have sought an interview with Cromwell;
but, as the request was not granted, Howgill addressed an epistle to him, in which
he says, that, having been unable to speak
to him, he was moved to write.   He assures
him, that, though he had been chosen and
exalted to rule, yet that, unless he abrogated
the laws concerning religion, by which the
people who were dear in the Lord's sight
were oppressed, and unless he ceased to
stint the eternal Spirit, his power should not
be established, but that he should be trodden
down in the mire, or scattered as dust before
the wind.   What notice was taken of this
epistle, we are not told.   But as to laws
concerning religion, says Sewel, none were
made in Cromwell's time to constrain people
to frequent the worship of the public or na-
tional Church, but there were many existing
laws which he allowed to remain unaltered,
and by which Quakers "were imprisoned

for refusing to swear, or for not paying tithes to maintain the priests; they were whipped like vagabonds for preaching in markets or other public places; or they were fined for not taking off their hats before magistrates, for this was called contempt of the magistracy; and when, for conscience' sake, they refused to pay such a fine, either the spoiling of their goods, or imprisonment, became their share."

Women, in various places, drew persecution on themselves by their strange conduct. At Bristol, one Elizabeth Marshall cried out in a church, after the preacher had pronounced the blessing, " Woe to those who take the word of the Lord in their mouths, and the Lord never sent them!" and to another preacher, on another occasion, "This is the word of the Lord to thee, 'I warn thee to repent, and to mind the light of Christ in thy conscience.'" Nor was she the only woman that thus annoyed the priests. In the same city Sarah Goldsmith, to testify against pride, clad herself in a coat of sackcloth, and walked, with her hair dishevelled, and dust strewn on her head, through the streets. At Norwich, two women named Elizabeth Heavens and Elizabeth Fletcher went about exhorting people, and, being brought before the justices, and paying them no due respect, were, though against the consent of the mayor, severely whipped.. At Great Torrington, Babara Loughton, behaving herself in a similar manner, was sentenced to like treatment.

At this time it was suspected that there was a plot against Oliver Cromwell, conducted by some Franciscan friars who had come from Rome, and who, as it was reported, were going about the country in the disguise of Quakers. Though there was no ground for this suspicion, yet it served as a pretence to the soldiery and magistrates for annoying and ill-treating the Quakers.

George Fox, after his peregrinations northwards, returned to Drayton, the place of his birth, to see his relations, from whom he had been absent three years. His visit is remarkable only for another dispute which he had with his old enemy, Nathaniel Stevens, the priest of the parish, a dispute at which George's father and brother were present. His father, though one of Stevens's congregation, was so well satisfied with George's arguments, that he struck his cane on the ground, and said, "Truly I see, he that will but stand to the truth, it will carry him out." His relations seem to have thought more favourably of his mental condition than they had thought previously; but George had recently abstained from any such exhibitions of himself as that which he had made at Lichfield.

He then went to Leicester, and from Leicester to Whetstone, where he was to hold a great meeting ; but before the people assembled, seventeen troopers of Colonel Hacker's regiment came to the ground, and, making George Fox prisoner, carried him before the colonel, who had also the major and some of the captains with him. The colonel spoke to him about the supposed plot against Cromwell, and George entered into a discussion with him concerning that and various other matters, not forgetting to enlarge on the light of Christ which enlightens every man. "Judas," observed the colonel, "was a disciple of Christ, and received, we may suppose, light from Him; was it that light which led him to betray his Master, and afterwards to hang himself?" "No," replied George, "it was the spirit of darkness, which was permitted to enter into Judas, and displace the light which had previously been in him."

The colonel then advised George to let his light guide him home, where it would be very proper for him to stay, and leave off going about to meetings. But George refused to make any promise that he would remain at home, saying that if he confined himself to his house, as in a prison, he would seem to acknowledge that he had been guilty of something wrong in going abroad; and that he should therefore go, if he should be moved, to, meetings, at which he and his friends would conduct themselves peaceably. " If such is your resolution, then," replied the colonel, " I will send you to answer for yourself to my Lord Protector, by Captain Drury, one of his life-guard."

On the following morning, accordingly, he was delivered to Captain Drury; but before they set out for London, he asked leave to speak again with the colonel, and being brought to the colonel's bedside, he was entreated by him again to keep away

from public meetings ; but George answered
as before, and the colonel repeated that he
must go before the Lord Protector.   George
then knelt down at the bedside, and prayed
the Lord to forgive him for acting like
Pilate, since he was set against him by the
priests as Pilate' was set against Christ by
the Jews.

CHAPTER XIII.

WHEN Captain Drury arrived with George
at London, he lodged him at the Mermaid,
near Charing Cross, and immediately proceeded to the Protector to give an account
of him. When he returned, he told George
that Cromwell required of him a promise
in writing that he would not carry a sword
or any other weapon against him or the
Government. George, without delay, wrote
an address to the Protector, whom he
styled simply Oliver Cromwell, declaring

that he had no design to bear a sword, or any other weapon, against him or any man, but that he was sent to testify against all war and violence. The Protector then signified that he wished to see George, who was accordingly conducted to him by Captain Drury, the following morning, at Whitehall, at so early an hour that Oliver was not yet dressed. George, as he entered, said, "Peace be to this house!" and, as he was fond of admonishing all men, high and low, he at once began to bid the Protector "keep in the fear of God, that he might receive wisdom from Him, that by it he might be ordered, and with it might order all things under his hand to God's glory."

"I spake much to him of truth," says George, in his account of the interview, "and a great deal of discourse I had with him about religion, wherein he carried himself very moderately. But he said we quarrelled with priests, whom he called ministers : I told him that I did not quarrel with them, but they quarrelled with me and my friends. 'But,' said I, 'if we own the prophets, Christ, and the apostles, we cannot hold up such teachers, prophets, and shepherds, as the prophets, Christ, and the apostles declared against; but we must declare against them by the same power and spirit.'" George then dwelt on the text, "Freely ye have received, freely give," and denounced all preaching for hire. He observed, too, that though all Christendom had the Scriptures, they wanted the spirit of those who gave forth the Scriptures, and that that was the reason why they were not in fellowship with the Son, or with the Father, or one with another. "As I spoke," says George, "he would several times say it was very good, and it was truth. Many more words I had with him, but, people coming in, I drew a little back, and, as I was turning, he caught me by the hand,

and, with tears in his eyes, said, ' Come again to my house, for if thou and I were but an hour of a day together, we should be nearer one to the other;' adding that he wished me no more ill than he did to his own soul. I told him if he did he wronged his own soul, and I bid him hearken to God's voice, that he might stand in his counsel, and obey it; and if he did so, that would keep him from hardness of heart; but if he did not hear God's voice, his heart would be hardened. And he said it was true. Then went I out; and when Captain Drury came out after me, he told me his Lord Protector said I was at liberty, and might go whither I would."

George was then conducted into a large hall, where there was a table set forth, and, on inquiring why he was brought thither, was told, in order that he might dine with the Protector's gentlemen. But George declined the invitation, and told them to let the Protector know that he would take nothing either of his meat or his drink. When Oliver heard this, he said, as George states, "Now I see there is a people risen and come up that I cannot win either with gifts, honours, offices, or places; but all other sects and people I can."

Whether Cromwell had heard of George's mad adventure at Lichfield, George's journal does not inform us.

During the time that George was confined at the Mermaid, priests, military officers, lay professors, and various other sorts of people, came in large numbers to see him. Some of them behaved to him with great civility, but others, and among them the Ranters, were troublesome, and occasionally insolent; and Colonel Packer, a Baptist, talked sometimes lightly and sometimes outrageously, but the Divine power, as George says, prevented him from doing mischief.

After Cromwell set him free, he and his adherents had great meetings in the city of London, the throngs of people being so great that he could scarcely make his way through them. He also went to Whitehall, and preached to those who were called Oliver's gentlemen or body-guard. Here he met with great opposition from a priest of the Independents, who spread many false reports about George, one of which was that he wore silver buttons, whereas George declares that they were but "alchemy." But George had, notwithstanding, great success, and converted some in the Protector's house and family; the Protector himself he was prevented from visiting again by the rudeness of the officers.

He, however, admonished him by a letter, warning him to beware of his own wit, craft, and policy, and of seeking any by-ends to himself; and he was moved at the same time, when his hand was in, to address

an exhortation to the Pope, and all other
rulers in Europe, charging them to take
heed to their ways, and to be slow to per-
secute.

From London he travelled through
various parts of Bedfordshire, Kent, Sussex,
and other southern counties. At Reading,
he called a meeting, at which many Baptists and Ranters presented themselves, and
entered into violent disputes with George
and his friends. The Ranters, who pleaded
against George's doctrine of endeavouring
after entire sinlessness, asserted, among
other affirmations, that God made the devil;
but this George denied, and argued that
the devil had become a devil by going out
of truth; "For God," said he, "made all
things good, and blessed them, but God did
not bless the devil."

CHAPTER XIV.

Travels with Hubberthorn—Ill received by the students at Cambridge—Oath of abjuration—Visits
Drayton again—Disputes with Baptists—George's
girdle—Brings himself into trouble by distributing
papers in Cornwall—Is apprehended, and sent to
Launceston gaol — Meeting with Desborough —
George keeps his hat on before the judge at the
assizes — Falsely accused by Major Ceely—Sentenced to pay a fine for keeping on his hat, or go to
prison.

THE reader may remember that George had
a horse when he was in the North, and left
him behind, on one occasion, apparently for
no very good reason.   We hear no more of
his having a horse till we find him riding
about in the county of Norfolk, in company
with Richard Hubberthorn, one of his
zealous supporters. One evening, they were

at an inn, at some town which he does not name, about thirty miles from Lynn, and had ordered the hostler to have their horses ready by nine the following morning, in order that they might pursue their way thither. But whilst they were in bed, there came, about eleven o'clock, a constable and officers, with authority to search for two horsemen, who rode upon grey horses, and were dressed in grey clothes, and were suspected of having robbed a house. George and Hubberthorn protested their innocence, but were, nevertheless, carried in the morning before a justice of peace that lived five miles distant. When they came into his presence, he was very angry because they did not take off their hats to him; but George said that he had kept his hat on before the Protector, who was not offended at it, and asked him why he should be offended, who was but the Protector's servant? Whether their hats were taken

off by force, or whether they were allowed
to keep them on, George does not tell us;
but the examination was proceeded with,
and the justice was reluctantly obliged to
acknowledge that they were not the men
against whom the warrant had been issued.
This annoyance was brought upon George
by one Captain Lawrence, an Independent,
who had heard him hold forth when he was
at the Mermaid, in London, and had been
offended by his remarks on the Independent
sect.

Visiting Cambridge in company with
Amor Stoddart, another of his supporters,
he was treated with exceeding rudeness
by the students, who gathered about him
in great numbers; but he rode through
them in the Lord's power, and kept on
his horse's back, while Amor Stoddart,
who had a less firm seat, was unhorsed.
When they were in the inn, the students

were so rude about the house, "that miners, colliers, and carters," says George, "could not have been ruder," the cause of their violence being that George was against their trade, the trade of preaching, to which they were apprenticed, so that they raged like Diana's craftsmen against Paul. The mayor incurred their displeasure by protecting George, but secured him and Stoddart a quiet night; and the next morning they rose at six, and escaped from the town before the students had quitted their beds.

The next year, 1655, came forth the oath of abjuration against King Charles, and many of the Quakers, who refused to swear for conscience' sake, suffered much on that account; and George, in consequence, addressed another epistle to the Protector, entreating him to adopt measures for the relief of the persecuted.

He complains sadly that the Protector hardened himself against all such applications.

Soon afterwards he paid another visit to his native town of Drayton, where he appears to have been kindly received by his relatives, and to have been left unmolested by others. Resuming his travels, he passed through various parts, and came at length to Dorchester, where he alighted, for he seems now to have constantly used a horse, at an inn that was kept by a Baptist. Induced, apparently, by the landlord, he requested the Baptists of the town to let him have their chapel for a place of meeting; but the Baptists refused. George then sent them word that any of them that liked might come to the inn; and some of them came, when a great dispute arose between them and George about baptism. George asked them whether they were sent to baptize as John was, and whether they had the same power that the apostles had. They admitted that they had not. He then asked them how many powers there are, whether there are any more than the power of God and the power of the devil. They said that there were not. Then, said George, if you have not the power of God, you act by the power of the devil. The sober people who were present said that the Baptists had thrown themselves on their backs. Next morning, as George and his friends were departing, the Baptists came forth to shake off the dust of their feet against them.

"What!" said George, "in the power of darkness! We, who are in the power of God, shake off the dust of our feet against you."

At Topsham, in Devonshire, he met with a very rude innkeeper. George wore a girdle, which, when he quitted the inn, he left, through forgetfulness, behind him. He sent to the innkeeper for it, who refused to restore it. Afterwards, when he was uneasy in his mind about it, he burnt it, lest, as he said, he should be bewitched by it; but after he had burnt it, he was more uneasy in mind than before.

As George was journeying towards St. Ives, he gave one of his admonitory papers, which he was very fond of distributing, to a friend, who chanced to hand it to a man that was servant to Major Ceely, a justice of the peace at St. Ives. This man gave the paper to his master, who, being no friend to George and his followers, sent the constables to bring them before him. Having asked George whether the paper was his, and George having owned it, he tendered George and his companions, Edward Pyot and William Salt, the oath of abjuration, when George drew forth the answer that he had given to the Protector. He then examined them severally, and a young priest who was present asked him many frivolous questions, especially about his hair, which was very long, and which, he said, he "was not to cut," though many had expressed displeasure at its length. The examination ended in the party being committed to a guard of soldiers, and despatched to the custody of Captain Fox, governor of Pendennis Castle, or, if he should not be at home, to Launceston gaol.

The soldiers were under the command of a Captain Keat, who, when they halted at Falmouth, allowed a brother of his to strike and ill-treat George. George remonstrated, and said, "Keat, dost thou allow this?"

"Yes," said Keat, "I do allow it."

George then appealed to the constables

of the town, who were very kind to George and his friends, and obliged the soldiers to show them civility. The constables also told George that Major-General Desborough was coming into those parts, who, they thought, would set George at liberty, if application were made to him. Near Bodmin, accordingly, they met General Desborough; and the captain of his troop, who rode before him, knew George and said,

"O Mr. Fox, what do you here?"

George gave an account how he was made prisoner.

"I will speak to the general, then," said he, "on your behalf," and, riding up to Desborough's coach, repeated what he had heard from George, who also added his own narrative. Desborough seems to have been well enough inclined to rescue George, but spoke slightingly of his inward light. George therefore began to reprove

him, and Desborough, not caring to listen
to George's admonitions, told the soldiers
that they might proceed with their prisoners to Launceston, as he could not stay
longer lest his horses should take cold.

When they were lodged in the gaol,
the gaoler required them to pay seven
shillings a week for the keep of their
horses, and seven shillings a week for
their own diet, a demand to which they
appear to have agreed.

They had to lie nine weeks in prison
before the assizes came on, at which Judge
Glyn, the chief justice of England, presided.   When they were brought into
the court, they stood with their hats on,
and George was moved to say to the
assembly, "Peace be amongst you!"

"Who are these that you have brought
into court?" asked Judge Glyn of the
gaoler.

"Prisoners, my lord," replied the gaoler.

"Why do they not put off their hats, then?" inquired the judge.

But the prisoners gave no heed to the intimation.

"The court commands you to put off your hats," said the judge.

"Then," says George, "I spake and said, 'Where did ever any magistrate, king, or judge, from Moses to Daniel, command any to put off their hats when they came before them in their courts, either amongst the Jews, the people of God, or amongst the heathens? And if the law of England doth command any such thing, show me the law either written or printed.'

"Then the judge grew very angry, and said, 'I do not carry my law-books on my back.'

"'But,' said I, 'tell me where it is written in any statute-book, that I may read it.'

"Then said the judge, 'Take him away, prevaricator!'

"So they took us away, and put us among the thieves. Presently after he calls to the gaoler, 'Bring them up again.'

- "'Come,' said he, 'where had they hats from Moses to Daniel? Come, answer me; I have you fast now.'

"I replied, 'Thou mayest read in the third of Daniel, that the three children were cast into the fiery furnace by Nebuchadnezzar's command, with their coats, their hose, and their hats on.'

"This plain instance stopped him, so that, not having anything else to say, he cried again, 'Take them away, gaoler.'"

They were, however, after a time, brought up again, and George, seeing several people taking oaths, was deeply concerned at such profanity, as he thought it, and was moved to circulate through the court some copies of a paper, which he had about him, against swearing. A copy reached the hands of the judge, who called it seditious, and asked George whether he were the author of it. George desired that it might be read, that he might hear it, and said that if it were his, he would own it and stand by it. In this request he was guilty of something like prevarication. The judge at first refused, but George reiterated his wish that it should be read, in order that the whole country might hear it, and judge whether there was any sedition in it or not, declaring that if any were found, he would willingly suffer for it. At length the judge allowed the clerk to read it, and, when he had concluded, George acknowledged that the paper was his, and proceeded to justify what it contained, and to lecture the court upon it. He was not of course allowed to proceed long; the judge told the gaoler to take off the hats of the prisoners. The gaoler did so, and gave them to the prisoners, who put them on again. George commenced another dissertation on hat-honour, which he ended with a request that the judge would make them some amends for their nine weeks' unjust imprisonment. But the judge, instead of complying with this request, ordered an indictment to be read, framed against George Fox, Edward Pyot, and William Salt, and charging them with various unlawful proceedings. Major Ceely, too, brought an accusation against Fox so monstrously false that it seems incredible that he could ever have made it. Yet there is such an air of truth running through Fox's journal, and he tells so many things against himself which he might have suppressed, that we can hardly suppose him ever to have told that which was not, and can scarcely do otherwise than trust his word in the present instance. Ceely said that George had taken him aside, and told him that he might be very serviceable for a design which he had in view, and which was, to involve the nation in civil blood-shed, and bring in King Charles, for which purpose he could raise forty thousand men at an hour's warning. Ceely added that he had a witness to swear to the truth of this charge; but the judge, who probably thought the charge chimerical, showed no alacrity to examine the witness. George then begged that his mittimus might be read to the court, and this, after some demur on the part of the judge, was allowed to be done, one of the three prisoners reading it aloud. From the mittimus it appeared that George and his two companions might have gone free if they had not refused to give sureties for their good behaviour; and George asked the judge whether it were likely that, having such a design in contemplation, he would have allowed himself to be taken to prison instead of giving sureties. The judge took no further notice of the accusation.

Major Ceely then made a facetious charge against George.

"May it please you, my lord," said he, "this man struck me, and gave me such a blow as I never had in my life."

"Art thou not ashamed," said George, "thou, a justice of the peace, and major of a troop of horse, to say that I, a prisoner, struck thee? Who is thy witness, and where did it take place?"

Ceely replied that it took place on the Castle-green, and that Captain Bradden, who was in court, was standing by. George called upon Captain Bradden to state whether he had seen anything of the kind. Captain Bradden was silent, and the judge, weary of the affair, ordered the gaoler to take away the prisoners, and, as they were removed, laid a fine upon them of twenty marks each for contempt of court in not taking off their hats, ordering that they should be kept in prison till the fine should be paid.

At night Captain Bradden came to visit George, and seven or eight justices with him, who all said that neither the judge nor anybody in court gave any credit to the charges which Major Ceely had brought against George. George then asked Captain Bradden why he had not testified to his innocence, as he had seen no blow given.

"Why," said Captain Bradden, "you will recollect that, when you were on the Castle-green, Major Ceely and I passed you, and the major took off his hat to you, and said, 'How do you do, Mr. Fox? Your servant, sir.' You then said to him, 'Take heed of hypocrisy, Major Ceely; for when came I to be thy master, and thou my servant? Do servants use to

cast their masters into prison?'   This was
the great blow that you gave him." George
then remembered that he had used those
words, and saw that Major Cecly had repre-
sented the figurative as real.

CHAPTER XV.

George's sufferings in Launceston gaol—Some relaxation—A friend offers to lie in prison in his stead—George reprimands Desborough and others—He is released, after seven months' confinement.

"THE assize being over," says George, "and we settled in prison on such a commitment that we were not likely to be soon released, we broke off from giving the gaoler seven shillings a week apiece for our horses, and seven shillings a week for ourselves, and sent our horses out into the country; upon which the gaoler grew very wicked and devilish, and put us down into Doomsdale, a nasty stinking place, where they used to put witches and murderers after they were condemned to die. The

place was so noisome that it was observed
few that went in did ever come out again
in health." The floor, as George describes
it, was all like mire, and the water in parts
rose above the top of the shoes, the whole
place not having been cleaned for several
years. The gaoler would not suffer them to
cleanse it themselves, nor allow them beds
or straw to lie on. Some people of the town,
on the first night of their confinement,
brought them a candle and a little straw,
which they set on fire to dispel the stench.
But the smoke went up into a room above,
where the gaoler was sleeping, and annoyed
him so much that, in a rage, he threw
down a quantity of refuse on their heads
through a hole in the ceiling, and so be-
spattered them that they were objects of
disgust to themselves and to each other,
and, with the smoke and the stench, were
in danger of being smothered and choked.
They were forced to stand all that night,

and were kept in that condition "a great while" before the gaoler would suffer them to cleanse the place, or to receive any food but what was given them through the grate.

This state of things, with but a slight change for the better, seems to have continued with them till the general quarter-sessions came on, when they drew up an account of their sufferings, and sent it to the justices at Bodmin, who ordered that they should have liberty to cleanse their prison, and to have their meat bought in the town. They also sent a narration of their hardships to the Protector, stating how they had been arrested by Major Ceely, and ill-treated by Captain Keat; and the Protector sent down an order to Major Fox, of Pendennis Castle, to examine into the affair. Captain Keat and his kinsman, who struck George, were in consequence cited before the authorities, and greatly censured; and

George was told that if he would change his principles, and make a charge against them on oath, he might recover large damages of them.

At last they had liberty to walk on the Castle-green, and were allowed to have a young woman, one Anne Downer, from London, to buy and dress their meat for them.

While George was still in confinement, a friend of his went to Oliver Cromwell, and offered to lie in prison for him, if he would allow George to go free. Cromwell was struck with the application, and said to those of his council who were about him, "Which of you would do as much for me, if I were in the same condition?" He would not grant the application, as it was contrary to law; but not long afterwards he directed General Desborough to communicate with the prisoners, and Desborough offered them their liberty if they would promise to go home and preach no more; but they would give no such promise.

. They were visited at times by justices and others, among whom was Captain Fox, the governor of Pendennis Castle, who, after looking George in the face, without speaking to him, turned to those that were with him, and said, "I never saw a simpler man in my life!" George, overhearing him, said, "Stay, we will see who is the simpler man." But Captain Fox walked off.

Major Desborough was fond of playing at bowls with the justices on the Castle-green, and several of the Quakers of the town went to him and his companions, to remonstrate with them on spending their time in such vanities, and seeking only their own pleasures, while they kept the servants of God in prison. But Desborough took little heed, and at last went off, leaving the settlement of the business to Colonel Bennett, who had the command of the gaol. Bennett offered to set them at liberty if they would pay the gaoler's fees, but they refused, both because they had been unjustly imprisoned, and because they had been ill-treated by the gaoler. Bennett insisted for a long time, but at last, says George, " The power of the Lord came so over him, that he freely set us at liberty." They left the prison on the 13th of September, 1656, having been in confinement more than seven months. Fox was now in the thirty-second year of his age.

CHAPTER XVI.

FROM Launceston he took his way through the southern counties to Exeter, and from thence to Bristol, preaching and exhorting. From Bristol he proceeded through Marlborough, Newbury, and Reading, to Kingston.

Riding from Kingston to London, with some of his friends, he observed, as he drew near Hyde Park, a great concourse of people, and soon after saw the Protector coming towards him in his coach. George rode up

to the side of the coach, when some of the
guards would have driven him back, but
the Protector told them to let him stay.
George accordingly rode by the coach-side
with him, declaring what he felt moved
to say to him of his condition, and of the
sufferings of the Quakers throughout the
country, and show how contrary persecution
was to the spirit of Christianity.   The Protector appears to have listened in silence,
and when they came to St. James's Park
gate, and George was parting from him, he
expressed a desire to see George at his
house.

A short time after, therefore, George, accompanied by Edward Pyot, went to Whitehall, where they found the Protector in
company with Dr. Owen, Vice-chancellor of
Oxford.   George was moved, as before, to
speak of the unhappy condition of the
Quakers, and then proceeded to discourse of
" the light that enlighteneth every man that

cometh into the world." Cromwell said that the light of which they spoke was merely natural light. George replied that it was "a divine light, proceeding from Christ the spiritual and heavenly man." George was standing by the table, and Cromwell came and sat upon the table beside him, observing jocularly, that he would be as high as George was. He continued to speak against George's light, and at last went away with a very unconcerned air. "But," says George, "the Lord's power came over him, so that, when he came to his wife and other company, he said, 'I never parted so from them before;' for he was judged in himself."

Leaving London, George made a journey to the north, as far as York, and returned through Warwick and Oxford to London again. At Oxford he found the students, as he had found those of Cambridge, very rude and troublesome.

He felt moved, he says, after his release

from Launceston gaol, to travel over most parts of the nation, in order to establish the truth, and to answer such objections as envious priests and professors were still raising against his doctrine. He was prompted to declare that those who pronounced the Friends to be antichrists were themselves antichrists, such as it was prophesied would come in the latter days, having sheep's clothing, but being inwardly ravening wolves. He testified that he was sent to preach again the everlasting Gospel, " which had been preached before to Abraham, and in the apostles' days," since which time there had been an apostasy. He showed that the Levitical priesthood was at an end, and that men ought therefore no longer to pay tithes to maintain priests. He argued that the apostle Paul discouraged baptism, for, when the converts divided into sects about it, some exulting in having been baptized by Paul, and others by

Apollos, he thanks God that he had not baptized more, indicating plainly that he would discontinue baptism, and that he considered himself sent, not to baptize, but to preach the Gospel. As to the eucharist, he observed that the celebration of it was not enjoined upon Christians, as was supposed, for Christ, according to St. Paul, who delivered to the Corinthians what he had received, used the words, " As often as ye eat this bread and drink this cup, ye do show the Lord's death till He come," and, " This do ye, as oft as ye drink it, in remembrance of Me," proving, by the expression "as often as," that people were not required to " do this" in perpetuity, but were left at liberty to do it or not as they should think proper. Christians, he said, were to seek the things that are above, the bread of salvation, which is not earthly bread, and the cup of salvation, which is not of earthly wine. Thus, says he, the objections which were raised against the Friends were answered, and the stumbling-blocks which were laid in the way of the faithful were removed.

But among the many converts to what George called truth, there were many sufferers, for he says that at the time when he was set free from Launceston gaol there were seldom fewer than one thousand of the Friends in prison, some for not paying tithes, some for absenting themselves from the steeple-houses, some for refusing to take oaths, and some for contempt of courts of justice in not taking off their hats.

During the remainder of this year, and during that which followed, George continued to ride through the country from town to town, holding meetings and delivering discourses. But he had more converts in the northern than in the southern parts. In 1659 there was a great drought, and Cromwell proclaimed a fast to be held throughout the nation; "and it was observed," says George, "that as far as truth had spread in the north, there were pleasant showers and rain enough, while in the south, in many places, they were almost spoiled for want of rain. At that time," he adds, "I was moved to write an answer to the Protector's proclamation, wherein I told him that if he had come to God's own truth, he should have had rain, and that drought was a sign unto them of their barrenness, and want of the water of life." Such was George's conceit, and such the obstinacy with which he set himself above all others.

One of his companions at this time was John Ap-John, a Welshman, who, at Tenby, was put into prison for standing with his hat on in the church, but released after a while at George's intercession. From another place he was expelled for haranguing the people in the streets. Throughout Wales they were greatly annoyed by dishonest hostlers who stole their horses' oats.

At one time their finances were so reduced that they had but one groat left between them; how they got a supply, George does not relate.

From Wales he passed through Chester to Liverpool, where he held a meeting, which was tolerably quiet. From thence he went to Manchester, at which he called another meeting, where he and his colleague were terribly pelted with stones, coals, and clods of earth, and had water thrown over them. At last the justices, who were then holding the sessions, sent officers, in order to quell the disturbance, to fetch George and John Ap-John before them. George, at his entrance into the court, seeing the people in a state of excitement, began, according to his practice, to admonish the magistrates on the propriety of teaching the people civility. The justices took his admonitions quietly, and, thinking that there was little harm in the prisoners, desired a constable to see them to their lodgings, and then let them go.

From hence George went northwards, and visited Carlisle, where he had suffered so long and troublesome an imprisonment; but on the present occasion he was not molested.

CHAPTER XVII.

GEORGE had for some time felt "drawings
on his spirit" to travel into Scotland, and
had had communications about going thither
with a Colonel William Osborne, of Scotland, who, in consequence, met him on the
borders and accompanied him into the country, being attended also by Robert Widders,
"a thundering man against hypocrisy and
deceit and the rottenness of the priests."

They proceeded by Dumfries and Douglas

to the Highlands, where Colonel Osborne lived, and where they stayed for some time and held meetings. They had great disputes with Calvinistic priests, who impressed upon their congregations that a certain number of them were doomed to everlasting destruction, and that, however devoutly they lived, they could never escape it. They had also great disputes with Baptists, who rose against them with logic and syllogisms; but George was moved, he says, "to thresh their chaffy light minds," showing their hearers that, by their fallacious way of discoursing, they might make white seem black, or prove "that because a cock had two legs, and each of them had two legs, therefore they were all cocks."

The priests grew exceedingly hostile to George and his party, and, assembling together, drew up in concert, as George relates, "articles of curses to be read in their several steeple-houses," ordering "that all the people should say Amen to them." Three of them George records in his journal:

"Cursed is he that saith, 'Every man hath a light within him sufficient to lead him to salvation;' and let all the people say Amen.

"Cursed is he that saith, 'Faith is without sin;' and let all the people say Amen.

"Cursed is he that denieth the Sabbath-day; and let all the people say Amen."

Several of the clergy also went to Edinburgh, with petitions to Oliver Cromwell's council there against George and his followers, praying that the promulgation of their doctrines might be prohibited. George went himself to Edinburgh at the same time. After holding a meeting, he found, on his return to his inn, an officer awaiting him with an order from the Scottish council, dated the 8th of October, 1657, citing him to appear before them on the fifth day after. The officer, having delivered the order, asked him whether he would appear or not. George gave no answer to the question, but inquired whether the order were genuine or counterfeit. The officer assured him of its genuineness.

At the time appointed George appeared before the assembly, and the doorkeeper, as he led him in, took off his hat, and hung it on a peg. George remonstrated, saying that he had kept on his hat before the Protector; but the doorkeeper was inflexible. After George had waited awhile, and nothing had been addressed to him, he was moved to say, "Peace be amongst you, and wait in the fear of God, that you may receive his wisdom from above, and order all things under your hands to his glory." When he ceased to speak, they asked him why he had come into Scotland.

He replied that he had come to visit the seed of God, which had long lain in bondage under corruption, and to bring the whole nation to the knowledge of the true light. They asked him whether he had any outward business in the country. He answered, No. They inquired how long he intended to stay. He replied that it would not be long, but that he did not know how long it would be, as the length of it must depend on his inward motions and suggestions. After causing him to withdraw a while, they called him in again, and told him that he must depart from Scotland in seven days. He asked them why, or what evil he had done, but they would give him no answer. He desired them to hear his justification, but they refused. He told them that Pharaoh heard Moses, and Herod heard John the Baptist, and that they ought not to be more unfeeling than heathens. But his words were of no avail, and he was forced to leave the council-room bursting in silence.

He paid little heed to the order to quit the country, and it is likely that the council cared little whether he obeyed it or not. He went back, with Colonel Osborne and Widders, and some others that had joined them, to the colonel's house in the Highlands, where, notwithstanding Osborne's protection, he met with but rude treatment from the highlanders, who on one occasion attacked him with pitchforks, and it was only by divine interposition, in George's opinion, that he escaped.

Leaving that part of the country, and going round by Perth and Stirling, he came again to Edinburgh, where an innkeeper told him that a warrant had been issued by the council for his apprehension, because he had not left the country on the expiration of the seven days. George rejoined that he did not care for a cartload of warrants ; and, indeed, no one offered to molest him. He was then moved to go back to Perth, where one Captain Davenport was favourable to the Friends, and to Perth he went. This Captain Davenport became afterwards so strong a Quaker that he lost a valuable appointment for not taking off his hat to his superiors, and addressing them with "thee" and "thou."

Having held a meeting in Perth, he hastened again to Edinburgh, and, as he rode up to the gate, he bade Robert Widders, who was with him, follow him; "and in the dread and power of the Lord," says George, "we came up to the two first sentries, and the Lord's power came so over them that we passed by them without any examination." Next day he was present at a meeting in the city, and was unmolested. He then proceeded to Dunbar, where he held the last meeting that he had in Scotland, and went away into England by Berwick.

From Berwick he travelled to Newcastle, and from thence to Durham, where he found a man come down from London to set up a college, in order to make, as he said, ministers of the Gospel. George immediately proceeded, with some of his followers, to reason with the man, and to make him see that to teach men Hebrew, Greek, and Latin, and " the seven arts," is but to teach after the way of the natural man, and not to form evangelical ministers. " For the languages," said George, " began at Babel ; and to the Greeks, that spake Greek as their mother tongue, the preaching of the cross of Christ was foolishness ; and to the Jews, that spake Hebrew as their mother tongue, Christ was a stumbling-block ; and as for the Romans, who had the Latin and Italian, they persecuted the Christians, and Pilate, one of the Roman governors, *set Hebrew, Greek, and Latin atop of Christ,* when he crucified Him. 'Now,' said I, 'dost thou think to make ministers of Christ by these natural confused languages, which sprung from Babel, and were *set atop of Christ*, the Life, by a persecutor?'" Such was George's reasoning, and it had, it appears, a powerful effect on "the man," for, "when we had thus discoursed with him," says George, "he became very loving and tender, and, after he had considered further of it, he never set up his college."

CHAPTER XVIII.

GEORGE now made his way, without any occurrence requiring particular notice, to London. Soon after his arrival there, he heard that a Jesuit, who had come over with the Spanish ambassador, had challenged any Quaker that chose, to dispute with him at the house of the Earl of Newport. He was willing, he said, to argue against the whole body of them, but, as it would be difficult and tedious to refute them all individually, he would match himself against

K

those of the wisest and most learned of them. George sent him word that he would meet him with Nicholas Bond and Edward Burrough. It was agreed that all that was asserted on either side should be considered nugatory, unless supported by Scripture. At the time appointed, George sent Bond and Burrough to commence the discourse, desiring them to ask the Jesuit whether the Church of Rome, in its present condition, was not degenerated from the true and primitive church, and destitute of the spirit and power which the church originally possessed. They asked the question accordingly, and the Jesuit replied that the Church of Rome still retained the purity of the primitive church. As he was maintaining this point, George came in himself, and, when he had concluded, asked him whether they had the Holy Ghost poured out upon them, as the apostles had. The Jesuit was obliged to confess that they had not.

" Then," said George, " if you have not the same Spirit descending on you as the apostles had, how can you be in the state in which the church was at the time of the apostles ? "

The priest was silenced on this head George then asked him what scriptural authority they had for establishing nunneries, abbeys, and monasteries, and for commanding to abstain from meats and marriage. The Jesuit said that they had the unwritten word, or tradition, for such practices. George demanded on what Scripture their tradition rested. The priest referred to the fifth verse of the second chapter of the first epistle to the Thessalonians, " When I was with you I told you these things." George observed that this was but a small and vague foundation on which to build so much, even if it could be fairly taken as referring to such observances, but showed that it was proved by the context to relate to quite other matters. They then disputed of transubstantiation, when George brought against it the ordinary arguments, which need not here be repeated. On the charge that the Church of Rome put men to death for religion, the Jesuit endeavoured to defend himself by saying that it was not the church that put them to death, but the civil magistrate. George silenced him by asking whether the magistrates did not act under the sanction of the church, and whether they were not themselves members of the church. The audience was highly pleased that George had the better in the contest.

About this time, 1658, it was rumoured that there were machinations in agitation to induce Cromwell to take the title of king; that these contrivances were secretly promoted by some who wished well to King Charles II., and who hoped that Cromwell, by such assumption, would alienate many of his partisans; and that the Protector himself was not averse to the title, but was prevented from taking it by the dissuasions of Desborough, Fleetwood, and Lambert. George Fox, as these reports spread, was moved to go to Cromwell, and warn him against yielding to the suggestions of pride. "He seemed to take well what I said to him," says George, "and thanked me." George was afterwards moved to write to him on the same subject. He also addressed, about the same time, a letter of consolation to Mrs. Claypole, who was then ill, and whose mind, he says, was stayed by his encouragement and exhortations.

During the period that many of the Quakers lay in prison, others of their sect made applications to the Parliament to be allowed to take their places in the gaols. But such requests were received with little favour; for the members, or their officers, would often threaten the Quakers who preferred these petitions that they would have them whipped and sent home. George remonstrated with the Parliament on these tyrannical proceedings in his usual style, but with little effect.

He then went to Hampton Court to speak to the Protector on the subject. This was his last interview with Cromwell. It is thus given in his own words :—" I met him riding into Hampton Court Park, and before I came at him, as he rode at the head of his life-guard, I saw and felt a waft (or apparition) of death go forth against him ; and, when I came to him he looked like a dead man. After I had laid the sufferings of Friends before him, and had warned him according as I was moved to speak to him, he bid me come to his house. So the next day I went up to Hampton Court again, to have spoken further with him. But when I came he was sick, and [Dr.] Harvey, who was one that waited on him, told me the doctors were not willing I should come in to speak with him; so I passed away and never saw him any more."

Cromwell died in the midst of a violent tempest, on the 3rd of September, 1658, the anniversary of his victories at Dunbar and Worcester, and his son Richard was proclaimed his successor.

George, soon after, had "a sight and sense" of the king's restoration, and so, he says, had some others. Some were so elated at the prospect of a change for the better, that they would have bought Somerset House to hold meetings in it; but George forbade them. A woman, who said that she had a revelation of the king's return, met George in the Strand, and told him that she must go to King Charles to declare it. George advised her to keep it to herself, lest she should suffer for treason; but "I saw," says he, "that her prophecy was true," for those in power were so exceedingly high-minded that he thought they must have a fall. One Thomas Aldam, a little before, had applied to Cromwell to release the Quakers from prison, and, on his refusal, had been moved to take his cap from his head, and to rend it in pieces before him, and to say to him, "So shall thy government be rent from thee and thy house." A female Quaker, shortly afterwards, walked into the assembled parliament with a pitcher in her hand, and, breaking it in pieces, told them that they should soon be broken to pieces in like manner.

Travelling to Reading, "I fell," says George, "into great grief and sorrow there, by reason of the great exercise that was upon my spirit; my countenance was altered, and I looked poor and thin; and there came a company of unclean spirits to me, and told me the plagues of God were upon me; but I told them it was the same spirit spake that in them that said so of Christ when He was stricken and smitten.

". . . . And then having recovered, and got through my travails and sufferings, my body and face swelled when I came abroad into the air; and then the bad spirits said I was grown fat, and they envied at that also: so I saw that no condition or state would please that spirit of theirs. But the Lord preserved me by his power and Spirit through and over all, and in the Lord's power I came to London again."

In London, however, he made no long stay, but resumed his travelling, and passed again through the southern counties. In some places he found the soldiers very troublesome at the meetings, and complaints of their conduct were made to General Monk, who, in consequence, issued the following order:

"St. James's, March 9th, 1659.

"I do require all officers and soldiers to forbear to disturb the peaccable meetings of the Quakers, they doing nothing prejudicial to the Parliament or Commonwealth of England.

"GEORGE MONK."

This prohibition proved of some effect in restraining the soldiers' disorderly behaviour.

CHAPTER XIX.

King Charles II. comes to the throne—George travels in the North—His perils—Visits Margaret
Fell, now a widow—Is apprehended at Ulverston
—His passiveness—Is committed to Lancaster
gaol—Disappointment of Major Porter, who committed him—Margaret Fell applies to Charles on
his behalf; and he is removed to the Queen's
Bench—Is discharged, through the influence of the
King—Charles is disposed to leniency towards the
Quakers, but many members of the Government
thwarted his wishes—Plot of the Fifth-monarchy
men—Extravagances of many Quakers.

About the time that Richard Cromwell
abdicated, and King Charles II. came to
the throne, George made another visit to
his relations at Drayton. How he was
received he has not told us.

He then travelled through the northern

counties. One of the places which he visited was Skipton in Yorkshire, where, he says, "there was a general meeting of men-Friends out of many counties, concerning the affairs of the Church. There was a Friend," he adds, "went naked through the town declaring truth, and he was much beaten;" a fate which he very well deserved, though George mentions the matter as nothing enormous or extravagant. "Some other Friends also," he proceeds, "came to me all bloody; and, as I walked in the street, there was a desperate fellow who had an intent to have done me a mischief, but he was prevented, and our meeting was quiet." So much better was the end than the commencement.

At a meeting at Arnside, in Lancashire, he met with a similar desperate fellow, who "was so outrageous that he would have cut Friends with an axe, but that he was restrained by some of his fellows." The same man set upon six Friends, as they were going to a meeting, and beat and abused them very much, bruising their faces, shedding much of their blood, and wounding them very sore, one of them in several parts of his body; "yet they lifted not up a hand against him, but gave him their backs and their cheeks to beat."

He then went to Swarthmore, to visit Margaret Fell, whose husband, Justice Thomas Fell, had died about two years before. While he was here, he was apprehended on a warrant from Major Porter, a justice of the peace, charging him with being a common disturber of the peace of the nation, an enemy to the king, and one of those who were desirous to raise a general insurrection and deluge the kingdom with blood. The constables took him to Ulverston, where they kept him during the night under a guard of sixteen men, for they had strange conceptions of his power to effect his escape. Some of them sat on the hearth and in the grate, lest he should fly up the chimney; and one of the constables said that he did not think a thousand men could have taken him. In the morning George put on his boots and spurs to ride with them on his own horse to the justice, but they took off his spurs and forced him to ride upon a horse smaller than his own, a multitude gathering about him with great rage and fury, and threatening him with extreme violence; but George looked on them very mildly, and said, "Here is my back, here are my cheeks; strike on." The mob, seeing him so passive, were ashamed to do him any serious harm. On the road the little horse began to fail, and George's horse being brought up, they allowed him to mount it; and at last they reached Lancaster, a distance of fourteen miles.

Here he was brought before Justice

Porter, who committed him to Lancaster gaol, on the charges set forth in the warrant for his apprehension.

George wrote and published a paper declaring his innocence of all that was laid to his charge, and Margaret Fell circulated another in support of it. Soon after, Margaret Fell determined to go to London, to apply to the king on George's behalf. Justice Porter, hearing of her purpose, set off to London to be beforehand with her; but, when he came to the court, he was so ill received, having been a great supporter of the Parliament, that he was soon glad to return into the country. The truth was, that he had thought to ingratiate himself with the king by imprisoning Fox, and was sadly disappointed at the result of his proceeding. When he came back from London, he was very willing to set George at liberty, but was unable, as he had ordered, in his warrant, that George should be kept prisoner till he should be released by the king or the Parliament.

After a short delay, Margaret Fell executed her intention of going to London, and was accompanied by Anne Curtis, the daughter of a sheriff of Bristol who had been hanged by the Parliament for engaging in a plot to restore the king. Charles, understanding whose daughter Anne Curtis was, received them both very kindly, and, when they interceded for George Fox, and requested that he might be brought to town, and heard before the court of King's Bench, their request was readily granted. Accordingly a writ of *habeas corpus* was immediately sent down to Lancaster; but the execution of it was retarded by so many delays and evasions, caused by officials who were no friends to the Quakers, that George did not arrive in London till two months afterwards.

He was brought before Judge Mallett,

the Chief Justice of the King's Bench,
who, finding that he had not been guilty of
any violence, and that the king wished him
to be set at liberty, made out his discharge.
But he was under restraint on this occasion, in gaol and otherwise, more than five
months.

During George's imprisonment, Richard
Hubberthorn had made application to the
king on the Quakers' behalf, and had been
granted an interview with His Majesty.
Charles questioned him, in the presence of
some of his lords, about the tenets of the
Quakers, and, being satisfied that they were
peaceably inclined, promised that they
should not be molested on account of their
opinions.   Some of the Quakers also were
admitted to the House of Lords, and were
allowed to state, in the presence of several
of the bishops, their reasons for declining
to pay tithes, to take oaths, and to join in
the worship of the Church; and all the

members of the House that were present listened with courtesy and attention. But as for the King's promise, says Sewel, he was, though a good-natured prince, so misled, that he seemed, in a short time, to have utterly forgotten to what his royal word had been pledged.

Seven hundred of the Quakers, however, who had been imprisoned under Oliver's and Richard's administrations, are said to have been set at liberty; and the king's government appear to have been inclined to grant the Friends freedom to worship in their own way. But there was always a party opposed to such concessions, who found means to have them delayed; and an insurrection of the millenarians, or fifth-monarchy men, which occurred in London at this time, and caused great disturbance and alarm, rendered the ministry, as well as the majority of the nation, less inclined to tolerance.

Many suspected that the Quakers were in league with the fifth-monarchy men, and George Fox, who was then in London, was arrested by some soldiers, and carried to Whitehall, where he was detained two or three hours, but was released on the interposition of an esquire of the king's bed-chamber, named Marsh. At his discharge, the marshal demanded fees; George replied that he would pay none, and expressed surprise that he should, ask fees of a man who was quite innocent, but said that he would, of his own free will, make him a present of twopence for him and the soldiers to drink. The soldiers raised a shout of derision. "Well," said George, "if you will not accept it, you may let it alone; but I shall pay you no fees." At length he was allowed to depart unmulcted.

Many Quakers, George Fox says several thousands, were thrown into prison in consequence of this insurrection; but as it did not appear that they were concerned in it, most of them were gradually set at liberty. It was also ordered that no soldiers should search any house unless attended with a constable. Margaret Fell, according to Fox's journal, was instrumental in procuring the Quakers indulgence. Fox himself, too, and others, wrote declarations, setting forth that they and their people were men of peace and quiet.

"God," says George, "heard the cries of his people, and brought an overflowing scourge over the heads of all our persecutors, which brought a quaking, and a dread, and a fear amongst and on them all, so that they who had nicknamed us Quakers, the Lord made them quake, and many of them would have been glad to have hid themselves amongst us; and some of them, through the distress that came upon them, did at length come to confess the truth. O the daily reproaches, revilings, and beatings we underwent amongst them, even in the highways, because we would not put off our hats to them, and for saying 'thou' and 'thee' to them! O the havoc and spoil the priests made of our goods, because we could not put into their mouths, and give them tithes!—besides casting into prisons, and besides the great fines laid upon us, because we could not swear! Yet some of them were so hardened in their wickedness, that, when they were turned out of their places and offices, they said, 'It was all along of us.' Wherefore I was moved to write to them, and to ask them, 'Did we ever resist you when you took away our ploughs and plough-gears, our carts and horses, our corn and cattle, our kettles and platters from us, and whipped us, and set us in the stocks, and cast us into prison, and all because we could not conform to your religions, manners, customs, and fashions? Did we ever resist you? Did we not give you our backs to beat, and our cheeks to pull off the hair, and our faces to spit on? Why then do you say that it was all along of us, when it was all along of yourselves, who followed your blind prophets that could foresee nothing of the times and things that were to come upon you, which we had long forewarned you of, as Jeremiah and Christ had fore-warned Jerusalem?'

"Many ways were these professors warned, both by word, by writing, and by signs; but they would believe none till it was too late. William Sympson was moved of the Lord to go out several times, for three years, naked and barefoot before them, as a sign unto them, in markets, courts, towns, cities, to priests' houses, and to great men's houses, telling them so should they be all stripped naked as he was stripped naked. And sometimes he was moved to put on hair sackcloth, and to besmear his face, and to tell them so would the Lord God besmear all their religion, as he was besmeared. Great sufferings did the poor man undergo, sore whippings with horsewhips and coachwhips on his bare body, grievous stonings and imprisonments, in three years' time, before the king came in, that they might have taken warning; but they would not, but rewarded his love with cruel usage. Only the mayor of Cambridge did nobly to him, for he put his gown about him, and took him to his house.

"Another friend, one Robert Huntingdon, was moved of the Lord to go into Carlisle steeple-house with a white sheet about him, among the great Presbyterians and Independents there, to show them that the surplice was coming up again; and he put a halter about his neck, to show them that a halter was coming upon them; which was fulfilled upon some of our persecutors not long after.

"Another, whose name was Richard Sale, living near West Chester, was moved to go to the steeple-house in the time of their worship, and to carry those persecuting priests and people a lantern and candle, as a figure of their darkness; but they cruelly abused him, and, like dark professors as they were, they put him into their prison called Little-ease, and so squeezed his body therein, that not long after he died."

Sadly obstinate and stiff-necked, and closed against conviction, did George consider those who refused to be warned by such signs and admonitions. William Sympson's imitation of Isaiah was a spectacle by which the founder of the Quakers deemed that all who saw it ought to have been edified and improved; and what monsters of iniquity must he have thought those who lashed with whips a man that appeared in such a condition, and shivered patiently in the east wind, for their good!

Travels of the Quakers to foreign countries; to Holland; to Egypt—George Robinson goes to Jerusalem—Mary Fisher to Constantinople—Her interview with the Sultan.

But England began now to seem too small a theatre for the Quakers' exertions. In 1661, "several Friends," says George, "were moved to go beyond the seas, to publish truth in foreign countries. John Stubbs, and Henry Fell, and Richard Costrop, were moved to go towards China and Prester John's country; but no masters of ships would carry them. With much ado they got a warrant from the king; but the East India Company found ways to avoid it, and the masters of the ships would not carry them. Then they went into Holland, hoping to have got passage there; but no passage could they get there neither. Then John Stubbs and Henry Fell were to go to Alexandria, in Egypt, intending to go by the caravans from thence. Meanwhile, Daniel Baker being to go to Smyrna, he drew Richard Costrop, contrary to his own freedom, to go along with him. And in the passage Richard falling sick, Daniel Baker left him sick in the ship, where he died; but that hard-hearted man afterwards lost his own condition.

"John Stubbs and Henry Fell got to Alexandria in Egypt, but they had not been long there before the English consul banished them from thence; yet, before they came away, they dispersed many books and papers there, for the opening of the principles and way of truth to the Turks and Grecians. They gave the book called 'The Pope's Strength

Broken' to an old friar, for him to give or send to the pope, which book when the friar had perused, he clapped his hand upon his breast, and confessed that what was written therein was truth; but, said he, 'if I should confess it openly, they would burn me.' So John Stubbs and Henry Fell, not being suffered to go further, returned to' England and came to London again. And John had a vision that the English and Dutch, who had joined together not to carry them, would fall out one with the other; and so it came to pass."

A young man, named George Robinson, felt a motion to travel to Jerusalem, to admonish the people there. He proceeded by Leghorn to St. Jean d'Acre, and from thence, with but little molestation from the Turks, to Joppa, where an Armenian merchant, who noticed his meek demeanour, showed him much kindness. At Ramoth the friars from Jerusalem came about him, and required him to conform to the practices of the pilgrims, by visiting the holy places and paying the usual tribute. As he refused to make any such engagement, they had him sent back to Joppa, and from thence to St. Jean d'Acre. But from this place he made his way back to Ramoth, where he was again seized by the friars, but was taken from them by some Turks, who hurried him into a mosque, and, after putting some questions to him, required him to adopt the Mahometan religion. To this demand he answered that he would rather die. They replied then that he should die, and were just going to burn him to death, when an old Turk, a man in authority, rescued him from them, and, seeing that he looked harmless, allowed him to live in his house for some days, where he discovered that he had been thrown into the hands of the Turks by a conspiracy of the friars. The malice of the friars was reported to the pasha, who obliged them to pay a fine, and to convey Robinson safely to Jerusalem. But when he arrived there, and the whole of the friars gathered about him, he seems. to have had very little to say to them besides exhorting them to turn from their evil ways, else the Divine anger would be kindled against them,—a message which he was moved to declare to them, whether they would hear or whether they would forbear. Having thus. delivered his mind, he felt himself at ease, and being conveyed, under the protection of the Turks, and at the expense of the friars, back to Ramla, he contrived to effect his return to England, and published an account of his adventures.

But the most remarkable expedition undertaken by a Quaker was that of Mary

Fisher to Constantinople, to admonish the Sultan Mahomet IV. She made her way to Smyrna, intending to go from thence to Adrianople, but was sent back, for some unknown reason, by the English consul, to Venice, from whence, being not at all daunted, she found another route to Adrianople, where she arrived at a time when the Sultan was encamped near the city with his army. She entered the camp alone, and sent notice, by some means, to the grand vizier, that an Englishwoman was come with a message from God to the Sultan. The vizier, from whatever motive, whether of seriousness or levity, had her brought before the Sultan the next morning, who received her in full divan. He asked her, first, through an interpreter, whether she had such a message to deliver as she had intimated. She replied "Yea," but seemed to hesitate, so that, thinking she might be unwilling to utter her mind before them all,

he asked her whether he should cause any
of his people to withdraw before she spoke.
As she answered in the negative, he desired
her to proceed, charging her to speak all
that she had to say from the Divine power,
as they were all willing to hear it whatever
it might be.

She then said what she had to say, but
what it was, neither Sewel nor any other
historian of her adventures has recorded.
When she had concluded, she asked the
Sultan whether he had understood all that
she had said, and he replied, "Yes, every
word," and added that what she had spoken
was truth.   He observed also that he could
not but respect a person who had come so
far with such a communication, and offered
to protect her if she would stay in his dominions, or to appoint her a guard to put her
safely on her way homewards, expressing his
wonder that she had travelled such a distance
without harm.   To remain in Turkey she

at once declined, and it does not appear that she accepted the offer of a guard. At the conclusion of the interview, however, the Turks had the curiosity to ask her what she thought of their prophet Mahomet. She answered, with something of the Quakers' caution, that she knew not Mahomet; that she knew Christ, who is the light of the world, and who enlightens every man coming into the world, to be a true prophet; and that they themselves might judge whether Mahomet was a true or false prophet from what he had spoken; repeating the text, " If the word that a prophet speaketh come to pass, then shall ye know that the Lord hath sent that prophet; but if it come not to pass, then shall ye know that the Lord never sent him." To this the Turks offered no contradiction; and Mary Fisher, having performed all that she desired, took her way from the camp to Constantinople, from whence she returned safely to England.

CHAPTER XXI.

George Fox, when he left London, proceeded to travel as before. He went first to
Bristol, and returned from thence through
London towards the north, till he came into
Leicestershire. When he was at Swanington, in that county, at the house of a widow
and her daughter, he was arrested one
evening by Lord Beaumont and a party of

soldiers, on pretence that he was holding a meeting. He was kept in confinement for the night, and brought up before Lord Beaumont, as a justice of the peace, on the following morning. George told him that he had been arrested contrary to law, as he was not holding any meeting. Lord Beaumont replied that he was well known, and not for any good, and asked him whether he would take the oaths of allegiance and supremacy. George answered that he would take no oath, having never taken one in his life; but this would not satisfy Lord Beaumont, who made out a mittimus for his consignment to Leicester gaol, on the ground that he and his party " were to have had a meeting."

As it was harvest-time, the constables who had the charge of George wanted to go to work, and were anxious to find some substitutes to go with him, and four others that were to be imprisoned under the same

mittimus, to Leicester. They would indeed
have given them the document to carry to
the gaol themselves, for this had been done
in many cases, the constables venturing, says
George, to trust the Friends, and believing
that if they promised to take their mittimus
to gaol, they would take it. But George
said that though the Friends had sometimes
done so, he was not inclined to take his own
commitment, but that somebody should take
it for him. At last they hired a poor
labouring man, who accompanied them to
the prison at Leicester, where they found
six or seven other Friends confined in a
dungeon in which there was scarcely space
for them to lie down. George with difficulty
procured a room, through the intercession
of William Smith, a Quaker of Leicester,
who came to visit him in the prison; and
was then told that whatever beer he required
he must take of the gaoler. George replied
that he would then do without beer, and

having obtained, apparently by means of the same friend, a pail of water and a little wormwood, mixed them together as a substitute for beer.

When the sessions came on, they were brought before the justices. The oaths of allegiance and supremacy were then again tendered to them; but George replied that neither he nor his friends would take them unless the justices could prove that after Christ and his apostles had forbidden swearing, they had again commanded Christians to swear. He then requested them to read the mittimus, which declared that they were sent to prison because they intended to have a meeting, and observed that they could not be legally committed unless they had been taken at a meeting. The justices, however, would take no notice of the mittimus, but indicted Fox and his companions for refusing to take the oaths of allegiance and supremacy.

The jury found them guilty; the justices remanded them to prison; and George and his party went out of the court, preaching along the streets. Shortly after they were lodged in the prison, the gaoler came to them, and said, "It is the court's pleasure that you should all be set at liberty." This was a sudden release; but it seems to have been due to the influence of Lord Hastings, from whom George, at the time that he was placed at the bar, had a letter in his possession, which, he says, he did not present to the justices, but intimates that they may have known Lord Hastings' pleasure from some other hand. Why he did not present the letter to the justices, he does not specify; but, after his discharge, he carried it to Lord Beaumont, who was somewhat abashed at it, yet blustered, and said that he would send him to prison again if he found him holding meetings at Swanington. However, his bluster was mere words, for George proceeded to Swanington and held a meeting unmolested.

After more peregrinations (for he had no home, and seems to have nowhere sought a resting-place, except for a few days) he went again to Swarthmore, where Margaret Fell still resided. Here he was told that Colonel Kirby, a justice of the peace, had been searching for him. George was moved to go to him, and ask him what he had to say.

"Why," said the colonel, "I have nothing against you; but I must warn you that Mistress Fell must not hold great meetings at her house, as they are contrary to the act of parliament." George observed that the act was directed against plotters of mischief, and contrivers of insurrection against the king, not against such as met at Margaret Fell's house, whom he knew to be his own peaceable neighbours. The colonel took the remark quietly, and shook George by the hand as he bade him farewell.

But shortly after, during Kirby's absence in London, a private meeting of the deputy-lieutenants and justices of the county was held at Houlker Hall, the residence of Justice Preston, when it was resolved to apprehend Fox. Fox heard of the meeting, and of a warrant being issued against him, soon enough to have allowed him to escape; but, as there was a rumour of an insurrection in the north, he thought that advantage might be taken of it to oppress his friends and adherents in his absence, and therefore resolved upon staying, that any intended evil might fall upon him rather than upon them. He accordingly appeared before the justices at Houlker Hall; and one of the questions put to him was whether he had any hand in the "Battledore."

The "Battledore" was a book that made its appearance while George was in Lancaster gaol, and was written to show that in all languages the pronouns *thou* and *thee* are properly used in addresses to single persons, and *you* in addresses to more than one. This was set forth by examples from the Scriptures, and from other books in about thirty languages. Two men named Stubbs and Furly were the chief compilers of it, and George himself made some additions. Copies of it, as George tells us, were presented to the king and council, to the two universities, and to the Bishop of London and the Archbishop of Canterbury. The king said that the language which the book advocated was the proper language of all nations; and "the Archbishop of Canterbury, being asked what he thought of it, was so at a stand that he could not tell what to say to it."

George acknowledged, in reply to Justice Preston, that he had a hand in this book which posed the Archbishop of Canterbury.

Justice Preston asked him whether he understood languages. George answered, "Sufficient for myself," and then began to harangue, in his usual style, on the inutility of a knowledge of languages to edification ; "for the many tongues," said he, "began but at the confusion of Babel; and, if I understand anything of them, *I judge and knock them down again* for any matter of salvation that is in them." The justice turned to his colleagues with a smile, and said, "George Fox *knocks down* all languages."

Sir George Middleton, another of the justices, then told him that he was a rebel and a traitor. George struck his hand on the table, and replied that he deserved no such epithets, as he had never felt or expressed anything but good-will towards the king, and had suffered for refusing to bear arms in the service of the Parliament. "Did you ever hear the like?" said Sir George. "Nay," said Fox, "you may hear it again if you will; for as for yourselves, though you talk of the king, where were you, the whole company of you, in Oliver's days, or what did ye do then for the king?" They next questioned him whether he had heard of the plot. He replied that he had heard of it, but that he knew nothing about it. They, knowing that he had written to caution his followers against plotting, asked him how he came to write against it if he did not know the nature of it, or some that were engaged in it. He said that he had written to prevent forward spirits from running into such enterprises, and that he had sent copies of his paper, besides dispersing it through the northern counties, to the king and his council. Some of them said that he was adverse to the laws of the land. George replied that the object of his teaching was to make people mortify the deeds of the flesh, and render them good and peaceable citizens, in which character they would be obedient to the laws.

At last they had recourse to the old demand that he should take the oaths of allegiance and supremacy. When he refused, they were inclined to make out a mittimus to send him to Lancaster gaol, but, on conferring together, they came to the resolution of merely making him promise to appear at the ensuing sessions. Having given this promise, he was allowed to depart, and returned with Margaret Fell to her house at Swarthmore.

When the sessions came on, he appeared at them according to his engagement. He advanced to the bar with his hat on, and his ordinary salutation, "Peace be unto you!" The chairman, Rawlinson, asked him how he showed respect to the magistrates, if he refused to take off his hat to them. He answered, "By coming when they call me." They then questioned him as he had been questioned before, about the plot, and required him again to take the oaths of allegiance and supremacy. He declined, and Rawlinson then asked him whether he deemed it unlawful to swear,—a question which was put, as George observes, on purpose to ensnare him; for, by a recent act of Charles II., all who should say that it was unlawful to swear were liable to be fined or banished. George answered that swearing was forbidden both by Christ and his apostle James; and the justices, after some consultation, committed him to prison. As he withdrew, he said to the justice and the people, "Bear witness that I suffer for my obedience to Christ's command."

The act under which George was committed had been expressly directed against the Quakers, and was afterwards the cause of banishment to many of that sect. The king was too good-natured to approve it, but his assent to it had been wrung from him by his ministers.

George was kept in prison till the assizes, which commenced on the fourteenth day of March, 1663, when he was brought before Judge Twisden. After George had saluted the court, and his hat had been removed, he was asked to take the oaths of supremacy and allegiance, as on former occasions. He remonstrated, and admonished the judge that no man should be called in question for his religion, as long as he lived peaceably. The judge grew angry, and said, "Sirrah! will you swear?" George was annoyed at the word "sirrah," and told the judge that it became neither his grey hairs nor his office to give nicknames to prisoners. George seems to have delivered himself in a rather loud tone of voice, for the judge retorted, whether gravely or in jest, "I will not be afraid of thee, George Fox. Thou speakest so loud that thy voice drowns mine and the court's; I must call for three or four criers to drown thy voice. Thou hast good lungs." George rejoined that if his voice were five times louder, he would still lift it up in the cause for which he was arraigned. The conclusion, however, was, that, as he would not take the oath, he was sent back to prison till the next assizes.

Some time previously Margaret Fell had been sent to the same prison, and as she refused, like George, to take the oath, she was, like him, recommitted to confinement.

During his imprisonment George wrote sundry papers of admonition to the judges and magistrates, against calling names and other unseemly practices, and stimulated those of his sect to draw up an account of their sufferings, and submit it to the proper authorities.

In the month of August assizes were again held at Lancaster. Twisden was one of the judges, but George, on this occasion, was placed before Judge Turner. He was now indicted under the act against those who refused to take oaths. The indictment being read, George observed that there were many gross errors in it; but the judge would not hear him, and the jury brought in a verdict of guilty. George cried out that both the justices and the jury had forsworn themselves,—an exclamation which caused such confusion in the court that the pronunciation of the sentence was delayed. Magaret Fell was next brought to the bar, and also found guilty.

On the following morning, both George and Margaret Fell were brought up to receive sentence. Margaret Fell had counsel, who found many errors in her indictment; and the judge having acknowledged them, she was remanded. As for George, he had no counsel, being unwilling, he said, to let any man plead for him; but when the judge asked him if he had anything to allege why sentence should not be passed upon him, he replied that, though he was no lawyer, yet he had much to say if the judge would but have patience to hear. At these words the judge laughed and the court laughed, and the judge said, "Come, what have you to say? I dare say that it will not amount to much."

George then asked him whether the oath was to be tendered to the king's subjects, or to the subjects of foreign princes.

"To the king's subjects, assuredly," said the judge.

"Look, then, at the indictment," rejoined George, "and you will see that you have left out the word subject, and therefore, not having named me as a subject, you cannot sentence me to the penalties of the statute of *præmunire.*"

The judge then inspected the indictment, and consulted the statute, and acknowledged that it was as George had said.

M

George added that he had something else to offer in arrest of judgment, and desired the court to see on what day the indictment stated that the oath was tendered to him at the sessions.

The court looked, and found that it was on Tuesday, the 11th of January.

"Look at your almanacs, then," said George, "and see whether there be any such day in them."

They looked, and found that the eleventh day of January had fallen on a Monday.

"Then," said George, "are ye not all, justices and jury alike, forsworn men? The justices have sworn that they tendered me the oath at the sessions, and the jury have found me guilty of having refused it on a day on which no sessions were held."

The judge, to get over the difficulty, asked whether the sessions did not begin on the 11th, but was answered that they did not begin till the 12th.　The justices who were in court were in a great rage, and said that somebody must have introduced the error into the indictment to befriend George. The judge admitted that this was another grave objection.

"But," continued George, "I have not yet come to the end of my objections; for I will ask you, next, in what year of the king the last assizes, which are mentioned in the indictment, were held here."

The judge said, in the sixteenth year of the king.

"But the indictment," rejoined George, "states that it was in the fifteenth year."

The judge found that it was so, and the justices were again in a rage, and could not tell what to say. The judge bade them look whether Margaret Fell's indictment con-tained the same error, and they found that it did not.

"But I have yet another observation to make," exclaimed George: "I ask you whether all the oath ought not to have been inserted in the indictment."

"Undoubtedly," said the judge, "it ought all to have been inserted."

"Yet," replied George, "if thou wilt compare the indictment with the oath, thou wilt find that several words of the oath are omitted."

The judge acknowledged that this was another error.

"Nevertheless," continued George, "I have not yet done."

"Nay," returned the judge, "I have heard enough; you need say no more."

"Then," said George, "I desire nothing at thy hands but law and justice."

"You must have justice," replied the judge, "and you shall have law."

George then asked, "Am I at liberty, and free from all that has ever been done against me in this matter?"

"Yes," said the judge, "you are free from

all that has been done against you.   But
then," he added, "I can put the oath to
any man, and I will tender you the oath
again.   Give him the book," said he to the
officer of the court.

"As this is the book," cried George,
"which bids me not swear, why do ye not
imprison the book, rather than seek to imprison me?"

"Nay," returned the judge, "but we
will imprison George Fox."

To prison, after some further remonstrance from him, he was accordingly remanded, to lie till the next assizes.

CHAPTER XXII.

COLONEL KIRBY, however favourably he had expressed himself to George before, had now turned decidedly against him. "He gave order to the gaoler," says George, "to keep me close, and suffer no flesh alive to come at me, for I was not fit, he said, to be discoursed with by men. Then was I put up," he adds, "into a smoky tower, where the smoke of the other prisoners came up so thick that it stood as dew upon the walls, and sometimes the smoke would be so thick that I could hardly see the candle when it burned; and I being locked under three locks, the under-gaoler, when the smoke was great, would hardly be persuaded to come up to unlock one of the uppermost doors, for fear of the smoke, so that I was almost smothered. Besides, it rained in upon my bed, and many times, when I went to stop out the rain in the cold winter season, my shirt would be as wet as muck with the rain that came in upon me while I was labouring to stop it out. In this manner did I lie all that long cold winter till the next assizes, in which time I was so starved with cold and rain that my body was greatly swelled, and my limbs much benumbed."

At the following assizes, in March, 1665, he was again brought to the bar. The same two judges, Turner and Twisden, were on that circuit, but George was this time placed before Judge Twisden. The word "subject," as well as several other words of the oath, had been omitted in the indictment presented on this occasion, as on the former, and George proceeded to make similar objections; but the judge had little patience to hear, and cried "Take him away, gaoler; take him away." During his absence the jury gave a verdict against him. "But I was never called," says George, "to hear sentence given; nor was any sentence given that I could hear of." He was, however, kept in confinement as before.

At the same assizes sentence of *præmunire* was passed upon Margaret Fell.

Shortly afterwards, as George relates, Colonel Kirby and some other of the justices grew unwilling that he should remain at Lancaster, where he had given them so much annoyance by exposing their blunders in the indictments, and exerted themselves to procure his removal to some more distant place. Accordingly, about six weeks after the assizes were concluded, they obtained an order from the Government for his removal from Lancaster, which order was accompanied by a letter from the Earl of Anglesea, saying that, if George Fox was guilty of what was laid to his charge, he deserved no clemency or mercy. When he was brought out of the prison, he was so weak that he could scarcely walk or stand; Kirby was present, with the under-sheriff, and offered him some wine, which he refused. They then cried, "Bring out the horses;" but George, before he would mount, desired them to show him their order for his removal, as there had been, he said, no sentence passed upon him, nor had he been pronounced subject to the penalties of *præmunire*, and he was, therefore, not the king's prisoner, but the sheriff's. No order, however, would they show him, but lifted him on horseback, and hurried him away to Bentham, a distance of fourteen miles, lashing the horse occasionally, and making it frisk, when he was scarcely able to keep his seat. Whither they intended to carry him, they would give him no information.

At length they reached York, when he learned that he was to be conveyed to Scarborough Castle. In a day or two they arrived there, and he was put into a room with an unsound roof and a smoky chimney, so that he could have no comfort in it. "I was forced," he says in his journal," to lay out a matter of fifty shillings to stop out the rain and keep the room from smoking so much; but when I had been at that charge, and had made the room somewhat tolerable, they removed me out of it, and put me into a worse room, where I had neither chimney nor firehearth, and the room being to the sea-side, and lying much open, the wind drove in the rain

forcibly, so that the water came over my
bed, and ran about the room, that I was
fain to skim it up with a platter. And
when my clothes were wet I had no fire to
dry them, so that my body was benumbed
with cold, and my fingers swelled that one
was grown as big as two; and though I
was at some charge on this room also, yet
I could not keep out the wind and rain.
Besides, they would suffer few Friends to
come at me, and many times not any, no,
not so much as to bring me a little food;
but I was forced for the first quarter to
hire one of the world to bring me neces-
saries, and sometimes the soldiers would
take it from her, and then she would scuffle
with them for it. Afterwards I hired
a soldier to fetch me water and bread,
and something to make a fire of, when I
was in a room where a fire could be made.
Commonly a threepenny loaf served me
three weeks, and sometimes longer, and

most of my drink was water that had wormwood steeped or bruised in it."

Though none of his own people were allowed to see him, many clergymen, Papists and others, to whom he was an object of curiosity, obtained admission to him, and held long disputes with him concerning religious matters. During the latter part of his imprisonment, the governor, Sir Jordan Crosslands, was very friendly to him, and let him enjoy considerable liberty.

At last, when he had been above a year in confinement, he drew up a letter, containing an account of his sufferings, to the king, into whose hands it was put by Marsh, the gentleman of the bed-chamber, who had already befriended George. His Majesty, being persuaded, as indeed he had always been, that George was harmless, and adverse to plots and war, caused an order to be sent to the governor of Scarborough Castle for his release. He left the prison on the 1st of September, 1666, the day before the great fire broke out in London.

Of this fire, says George, the people of London were forewarned, though few believed the admonition; "for we had a Friend," he relates, "that was moved to come out of Huntingdonshire a little before the fire, and to scatter his money up and down the streets, and to turn his horse loose in the streets, and to untie the knees of his breeches, and let his stockings fall down, and to unbutton his doublet, and told the people so should they run up and down, scattering their money and their goods, half undressed, like mad people, as he was a sign to them." How incredulous must George and the man of Huntingdon have thought the people of London, who were slow to believe on such indications that a fire was going to happen! "Thus hath the Lord exercised his prophets and servants by his power, and showed them signs of his judgments, and sent them to forewarn the people; but instead of repenting, they have beaten and cruelly ill-treated some, and some they have imprisoned, both in the former power's days [the time of the Parliament] and since. Some have been moved to go naked in the streets, as signs of their nakedness, and have declared amongst them that God would strip them out of their hypocritical professions, and make them as bare and naked as they were. But instead of considering it, they have many times whipped or otherwise abused them, and sometimes imprisoned them. Others have been moved to go in sackcloth, and to denounce the woes and vengeance of God against the pride and haughtiness of the people; but few regarded it."

CHAPTER XXIII.

GEORGE now resumed his travels, but he had suffered so much from his long imprisonment, that he was for a long while weak and stiff in the joints, so that he could scarcely mount his horse; nor could he, for some time, endure to be near the fire, or to take warm meat.

About this time, with the aid of his preachers, he arranged quarterly and monthly meetings among the Friends. In Lancashire

he met Margaret Fell, who, though a prisoner, got liberty, he says, to come thither,
and accompanied him to Jane Milner's in
Cheshire, where they parted.

At Waltham he recommended that there
should be schools for girls and boys, to in-
struct them in whatever should be thought
useful.

Going to London, he visited his friend
Marsh, whom he found at dinner. He
would have had George sit down with him
at the table, but George " had not freedom
to do so." He stayed, however, and had
some dispute with a Papist who was there.
When the dinner was ended, Marsh, who
was a justice of the peace for Middlesex,
took him aside into another room, and observed that, in the administration of justice,
he was often at a loss to make a distinction
between the Quakers and other dissenters :
" For," said he, " you cannot swear, and
the Independents, Baptists, and Fifth-mon-

archy men say that they cannot swear; and therefore how shall I be able to distinguish between you and them, especially as you and they all say alike that you abstain from swearing for conscience' sake?"

George replied that he would show him how to distinguish : "For they whom thou speakest of, or most of them, can and do swear in some cases, but we cannot swear in any case. If a man should steal their cows or horses, and thou shouldest ask them whether they would swear they were theirs, many of them would readily do it. But if thou try our friends, thou wilt find that they cannot swear even for their own goods. Therefore, when thou puttest the oath of allegiance to them and they refuse it, ask them whether they can swear in any other case. A thief stole two beasts from a friend of ours in Berkshire," continued George, "and the thief was taken and cast into prison; and the Friend appeared against him at the assizes. But somebody having informed the judge that the man that prosecuted was a Quaker, and could not swear, the judge, before he heard what the Friend could say, said, 'Is he a Quaker, and will he not swear? Then tender him the oaths of allegiance and supremacy.' So he cast the Friend into prison, and premunired him, and let the thief go at liberty that had stolen his goods." Marsh, on hearing this case, observed that the judge was a very wicked man. In his capacity of justice, Marsh was afterwards very serviceable to the Quakers, setting many of them, when they were brought before him, at liberty, or, when he could not avoid sending them to prison, sending them only for a few hours. At last he told the king that he could not conscientiously imprison any more of them, and, in order to resign his justiceship, removed out of the county of Middlesex.

George was now moved to visit Ireland, whither he sailed from Liverpool. On landing at Dublin, he thought that the air had an unpleasant smell, different from that of England; a smell which he imputed to the corruption of the country, and the blood which had been shed there in popish massacres.

His travels through Ireland require no particular notice, being very similar to those which he made through England, except that he met with more Papists to exercise his powers of disputation. The mayor of Cork was hostile to the Quakers, and gave George some annoyance, but did not succeed in getting him into prison. On his return he had a very stormy passage, being kept at sea two nights, but at last reached Liverpool in safety.

From Liverpool he travelled to Bristol, where he met Margaret Fell, who was on a visit to one of her married daughters there.

George was now about to take a very im-
portant step in life. How it was taken it
will be well to let him state in his own
words. " I had seen from the Lord," he
says, " a considerable time before, that I
should take Margaret Fell to be my wife.
And when I first mentioned it to her, she
felt the answer of life from God thereunto.
But though the Lord had opened this thing
unto me, yet I had not received a command
from the Lord for the accomplishing of it
then, wherefore I let the thing rest, and
went on in the work of service of the Lord
as before, according as the Lord led me,
travelling up and down in this nation, and
through the nation of Ireland. But now
after I was come back from Ireland, and
was come to Bristol and found Margaret
Fell there, it opened in me from the Lord,
that the thing should be now accomplished.
And after we had discoursed the thing together, I told her, if she also was satisfied

with the accomplishing of it now, she should
first send for her children, which she did.
And when the rest of her daughters were
come, I asked both them and her sons-in-
law if they had anything against it or for it,
desiring them to speak; and they all severally expressed their satisfaction therein."
Pecuniary arrangements had been made for
the children, it appeared, according to their
father's will. "I told them I was plain,"
adds George, "and would have all things
done plainly; for I sought not any outward
advantage to myself. So, after I had acquainted the children with it, our intention
of marriage was laid before Friends, both
privately and publicly, to the full satisfaction of Friends, many of whom gave testimony thereunto that it was of God. Afterwards a meeting being appointed on purpose
for the accomplishing thereof, in the public
meeting-house at Broadmead in Bristol, we
took each other in marriage, in the everlast-

ting covenant and immortal seed of life. In the sense whereof living and weighty testimonies were borne thereunto by Friends, in the movings of the heavenly Power which united us together. There was a certificate relating both the proceedings and the marriage, openly read and signed by the relations, and by most of the ancient Friends of that city, besides many other Friends from divers parts of the nation."

George says that in this marriage he " sought no advantage to himself." How he had lived down to this period of his life, his journal gives no indication. He had money, as we have seen, when he was in prison; he had a horse to ride when he was at large, and means to pay his traveling expenses; but from what sources he secured these accommodations, he is silent. Nor is it apparent how his wife was to be supported, unless on her own money.

After they were married, they stayed

about a week in Bristol, and then went together to Oldstone, where they took leave of each other and separated, Margaret going homewards to the north, and George setting out to travel through Wiltshire, Berkshire, and Oxfordshire, towards London.

In London he made but little stay, but proceeded into Essex and Hertfordshire, despatching a letter to his wife to say that he should soon be in Leicestershire, and would meet her there. But when he visited that county, he found that she had been seized in her house, and carried back to Lancaster gaol. George in consequence went back to London, to endeavour to procure his wife's release, but made no great haste, for he held "many large and blessed meetings" on the way. On his arrival, however, he sent Mary Lower and Sarah Fell, two of his wife's daughters, to the king, to solicit her discharge, which, with some difficulty, they obtained; and Sarah Fell, accompanied by her brother and sister Rous, carried the order for it immediately to Lancaster.

This Sarah Fell is said to have been a very remarkable woman. The Quakers extol her, says Croese, as having been not only eminently beautiful in person, but of extraordinary abilities and memory. She was so eloquent in her addresses and exhortations, and so fervent in her supplications to heaven, that she affected her audiences with wonder and admiration. She applied herself to the study of Hebrew, that she might be the better able to support the tenets of her sect from the Scriptures, and she acquired such a knowledge of the language that she wrote religious tracts in it. Two of her brothers, Leonard and Henry, were also eminent teachers in the society. In adopting this mode of life, they did but imitate their mother, who, when she fell under the influence of Fox, exchanged her spinning, and other household occupations, for the business of making proselytes, which she pursued not only orally, but by writing and publishing books; and her house became a seminary for students and preachers both male and female. William Caton, a promising young man, who had been taken into the family by Justice Fell as a companion and tutor to his eldest son, was so affected by the arguments and example of Fox and Margaret Fell, that he felt himself unable to continue Latin verse-making, or to take off his hat in salutation, so that he was soon qualified for a travelling teacher, and, instead of devoting himself to rational study, as his friends had expected, engaged in peregrinations, at home and abroad, that procured him numerous imprisonments, whippings, and other penalties.

About this time, in consequence of some

disturbances that had occurred at meetings of religious parties, and especially at one in Gloucestershire, where a Presbyterian preacher and the priest of the parish, with their partisans, had engaged in a fierce contest, in which the prayer-book was cut to pieces, and other gross outrages committed, an act of parliament was passed against conventicles, prohibiting more than five persons from assembling together for the purpose or on pretence of any religious exercise otherwise than in conformity with the liturgy and practice of the Church of England. On the Sunday after this act came into force, George Fox, who attended a meeting in Gracechurch Street, was in danger of being imprisoned, and was brought the following day before the lord mayor; but as his lordship was not inclined to severity, and as the mob frightened away the informer, he was allowed to depart.

Meetings, in spite of the act, continued to be held, and George himself was soon after present at several in Oxfordshire and Buckinghamshire.

During this year he fell ill at Stratford, near London, and was reduced to great weakness, so that he lost, he says, both his hearing and his sight for some weeks, and was not expected, by any that visited him, to recover. During his sickness he had many visions relating to all the religions of the world, and the people that lived under them, in which the priests that upheld them appeared as " men-eaters, eating up the people like bread, and gnawing the flesh from off their bones." He also saw the New Jerusalem, and the beauty and glory of it. His recovery was very slow.

He had expected that his wife would have been at liberty to visit him during his sufferings, but, in consequence of the increasing informations under the new act against conventicles, the authorities at Lancaster, though they received the order for her discharge from her daughter, found pretexts for detaining her in prison. At length, however, George was moved to send Mary Fisher, and " another woman Friend," to the king, to solicit her liberty, and, as they went in the faith, they found favour with His Majesty, so that her discharge was granted " under the broad seal, to clear both her and her estate, after she had been," as George says, " ten years a prisoner, and *premunired."*

This document George sent down to her by a friend, and wrote to her, at the same time, to say that he felt under a divine obligation " to go beyond the seas to visit the plantations in America," and to desire her " to hasten up to London, as soon as she could conveniently, after she had obtained her liberty," because the ship was then fitting out for the voyage.

His wife hastened up accordingly, and accompanied him to the Downs on the twelfth day of June, 1670. About a dozen of the most eminent among the Friends were with him, among whom were the notorious Solomon Eccles and Elizabeth Hooton.

CHAPTER XXIV.

WHEN they had been about three weeks at sea, they were chased by a Sallee rover, but outsailed her, and got safe to Barbadoes, where they were to make some stay. While they were at anchor here, there came in a Sallee merchantman, the crew of which told the people of the island that one of the Sallee rovers had seen a monstrous vessel at sea, and had kept her in chase till they nearly overtook her, but that there was a spirit in her which prevented them from capturing her. By this report George and his party were confirmed in a belief which they had conceived on the voyage, that they had been delivered by divine interposition from an enemy that was seeking to devour them.

George was not sea-sick on the voyage, but, from the effects of his previous illness in gaol and afterwards, was very weak and debilitated, so that, when he arrived in Barbadoes, he was obliged to confine himself for three weeks to the house in which he took up his abode. He found some Friends in the island, and one Thomas Rous, who lodged him for a time, borrowed a coach of Colonel Chamberlain, in which he was enabled to take the air. Some meetings of Friends were held at Thomas Rous's, at which George, as he began to regain strength, was able to preside. Some

of the Friends who came over with him
from England dispersed themselves through
the other islands.

He stayed in all three months in Barbadoes, and then, "feeling his spirit clear of
that island," and having " drawings towards
Jamaica," he proceeded thither, where he
was kindly received by the governor. Here
Elizabeth Hooton, who accompanied him,
and had now reached a great age, died.
His letters to his wife from these parts were
short, but apparently affectionate.

Having remained seven weeks in Jamaica,
he embarked on the 8th of January,
1672, for Maryland. On his landing, after
a passage of between six and seven weeks,
he was met by John Burneyate, a leading
man among the Quakers in that province,
who soon after called a meeting, which
proved, as George says, a great and heavenly meeting. He was moved, he adds,
" to send to the Indian emperor and his

kings to come to that meeting. The emperor came and was at the meeting; but his kings, lying further off, could not reach thither time enough, yet they came after." They heard what George said willingly, according to his report, and he desired them to speak to their people what he had spoken to them. The next day he and his companions set out for New England, proceeding on horseback through the woods and wildernesses.

Here it may be proper to notice how Quakerism was first introduced into New England. Two women, named Mary Fisher and Ann Austin, were the first of that persuasion who arrived there, having come in a ship from England, in the month of July, 1656, when George Fox was thirty-two years of age. As yet no law had been made there against Quakers, yet Richard Billingham, the deputy-governor, committed these two women to prison on their landing, as being of that sect, because one of them, in speaking to him, had said "thou" instead of "you." They were afterwards barbarously treated; they were undressed and searched, on pretence of ascertaining whether they were witches; they were kept in confinement five weeks, and almost starved; and at last the captain of a vessel was forced to carry them back to their country, and the gaoler kept their beds, which had been brought on shore, for his fees.

"Such was the entertainment," says Sewel, "which the Quakers first met with at Boston, and that from a people who pretended that, for conscience' sake, they had chosen the wilderness of America before the well-cultivated Old England."

Four male and four female Quakers, who landed about a month afterwards, were treated in a similar manner by John Endicott, the governor, and, after eleven weeks' stay, were shipped back to England. A law was then made prohibiting all masters of ships from bringing Quakers to New England, and Quakers themselves from landing there, under penalty of imprisonment.

Quakers, however, still continued to appear in that country, and most cruel measures were adopted for their exclusion, the Dutch settlers imitating the English in the severity of their enactments. At length two Quakers, William Robinson, a London trader, and Marmaduke Stevenson, an agriculturist from Yorkshire, both of whom persisted in frequenting Boston and the neighbourhood, were ordered by the court to keep themselves out of its jurisdiction "under pain of death," and, as they did not feel "free in mind" to obey the order, were, in the latter part of the year 1659, actually hanged, and their dead corpses were stripped and mangled by the hands of the mob. A woman, named Mary Dyar, was executed soon afterwards; and in the early part of the following year, two men, William Leddra and Wenlock Christison.

But these proceedings, which far surpassed in rigour anything that had been done against the Quakers in England, excited the attention of the English people, as well others as the Quakers themselves, and application being made to the king on the subject, a mandamus was addressed by the English government to the authorities in New England, directing that if there were any Quakers in that country under sentence of imprisonment, corporeal punishment, or death, the proceedings against them should be stopped, and they should be sent over to England to be dealt with according to the English laws.

This order was so far obeyed that the Quakers who were then in prison were set at liberty; and three deputies, Colonel Temple, a priest named Norton, and Simon

Broadstreet, one of the magistrates, were sent over to England to inform the king of their release, and to deprecate his displeasure. During their stay in England, George Fox and some of his friends found an opportunity of speaking to them, and charged them boldly—at least Norton and Broadstreet, who acknowledged that they were concerned in the persecution—with murder, in having, though subjects of England, put to death peaceable citizens, not by English laws, but by arbitrary enactments of their own; and many of the old royalists, says Sewel, were earnest with the Quakers to bring the New England persecutors, or as many of them as possible, to trial. But George replied that he would leave them to Him to whom vengeance belonged; and nothing accordingly was done in the matter.

It does not appear that any more Quakers were put to death in New England, but persecution was not discontinued; and ill-treatment of them, by whipping, imprisonment, and other modes of vexation, was at times indulged to a great extent.

At the time when Robinson and Stevenson were executed, George Fox was in Lancaster gaol, and had, as he says, a perfect sense of their sufferings, as if the halter had been put about his own neck, though he had not at that time heard of the affair. This was probably a fancy which entered into his mind after the news of the men's death had reached him, and which he has recorded in his journal as a sensation felt by him at the time when the execution took place.

When George arrived in New England, in 1672, the Quakers seem to have been tolerated there to much the same extent as in Old England. His journey thither from Maryland was not effected without great trouble, but ended safely.

To give a detailed account of his travels there and in the adjacent provinces, would be useless. They were of the same nature as his journeys through England; he called meetings, in concert with his companions, delivered addresses, and increased apparently the numbers of his sect, for "many were reached," in divers places, and "confessed the truth."

One incident which occurred when he was travelling through New Jersey, may very well be noticed. He had with him one John Jay, who, when they reached Shrewsbury, had to try a horse, and the animal, as he mounted, ran away with him, threw him over his head, and, as the spectators exclaimed, broke his neck. "They that were near him," says George, "took him up dead, and carried him a good way and laid him on a tree. I got to him as soon as I could, and, feeling on him, concluded he was dead. And as I stood by him,

pitying him and his family, I took hold
of his hair, and his head turned any way,
his neck was so limber. Whereupon, throw-
ing away my stick and my gloves, I took
his head in both my hands, and setting my
knees against the tree, I raised his head
and perceived that there was nothing out or
broken that way. Then I put one hand
under his chin and the other behind his
head, and raised his head two or three times
with all my strength, and brought it in.
I soon perceived his neck began to grow
stiff again, and then he began to rattle in
the throat, and quickly after to breathe.
The people were amazed : but I bid them
have a good heart, and be of good faith, and
carry him into the house. They did so,
and set him by the fire ; but I bid them
get him some warm thing to drink, and put
him to bed. After he had been in the
house awhile, he began to speak, but did
not know where he had been." The next

day he was able to travel, and "many hundreds of miles," adds George, "did he travel with us after this."

He seems to have met with no molestation during his travels. At one place, near Rhode Island, the people would have hired him, if they had had the means, to be their minister; but George, as soon as he heard of their notion, said it was time for him to be gone, observing that the Friends' principle was to discourage the hiring of ministers, and to bring every one to be his own teacher in himself.

At last, after having journeyed many miles, sometimes by land, and sometimes by water; after having forded many rivers, sometimes in boats and Indian canoes, and sometimes on foot, without shoes and stockings; and after having discoursed with numbers of his own people, and numbers of barbarians, with the aid of an interpreter, he returned to that part of Maryland whence he had disembarked the previous year. Here he went on shipboard on the 1st of March, 1673.

He found that, during his absence, Solomon Eccles, with whom he had parted at Jamaica, had, on coming from that island to New England, been made prisoner at a meeting, and banished to Barbadoes.

After a tempestuous voyage, in which the waves rose like mountains, so as to astonish even the crew of the vessel, George Fox reached Bristol on the 28th of April.

The reader may like to see in what terms he announced his safe arrival to his wife:

"DEAR HEART,

"This day we came into Bristol near night from the seas, glory to the

Lord God over all for ever, who was our convoy, and steered our course; who is the God of the whole earth, and of the seas and winds, and made the clouds his chariots, beyond all words, blessed be his name for ever! Who is over all in his great power and wisdom, amen. Robert Widders and James Lancaster are with me, and we are all well; glory to the Lord for ever, who hath carried us through many perils, perils by water and in storms, perils by pirates and robbers, perils in the wilderness, and among false professors; praises whose glory is over all for ever, amen. Therefore mind the fresh life, and live all to God in it. I do intend (if the Lord will) to stay awhile this way, it may be till the fair. So no more, but my love to all friends.

"G. F.

"Bristol, the 28th day of
the fourth month, 1673."

An easy, but extraordinary way of filling up a letter to a wife after a long absence.

Though he was content to stay away from Margaret till the fair, Margaret was not content to stay so long away from him. She came at once to join him at Bristol, with her son-in-law, Lower, and two of her daughters; and soon after her other son-in-law, John Rous, came down from London, with William Penn and his wife. At the fair time, when many people flocked to Bristol, they had "great and glorious meetings."

CHAPTER XXV.

HE soon quitted his wife, and travelled from place to place till he came to Kingston-upon-Thames, where she rejoined him. Proceeding to London, he found that the Socinians and Baptists had been busy in his absence, and had printed many rude books against the Quakers, which gave him great trouble to answer. But having succeeded in replying to some of them, either with his own hand or by the aid of others, he paid a visit to William

Penn at Rickmansworth, in Hertfordshire, where he was met by Thomas Lower, and went forward in company with him to Adderbury, in Oxfordshire. Here, as he was sitting at supper at the house of a man named Bray Doily, he felt that he was going to be made prisoner. He travelled onwards, however, into Worcestershire, and while he was at Tredington in that county, he was apprehended, by a justice of peace named Parker, for having held a meeting there, and committed with Lower to Worcester gaol. He made application to Lord Windsor, the lord-lieutenant of the county, stating that he had been unfairly imprisoned, not having been taken at a meeting, but after a meeting in a private house; but Lord Windsor would no nothing in his behalf. As for Lower, he might have obtained his release by the intercession of his brother, Dr. Lower, one of the king's physicians; but he chose rather to take his fortune with his father-in-law than to desert him.

In the month of January, 1674, they were brought to trial at the sessions at Worcester. Fox's treatment was much the same as he had experienced on previous occasions. After he had said what he thought proper in his defence, he was desired to take the oaths of allegiance and supremacy, and, on his refusal, was sent back to prison. As for Lower, he was discharged, because, according to Sewel, he was thought to have more protection at court than Fox had. On his release, he remonstrated with the justices for detaining Fox while they dismissed himself, but was told that he had better remain quiet, or they would put the oaths to him.

After the close of the sessions, a *habeas corpus* was sent to the sheriff of Worcester for the removal of George Fox to the King's Bench. Adopting the easy mode in which Quakers, as we have already seen, were often despatched to London, the sheriff made Lower his deputy, and sent Fox to London under his charge. When he came before the court, the chief justice was at first disposed to discharge him, yet, being afterwards swayed by some malicious representations of Justice Parker, resolved on remanding him to the prison at Worcester, to be tried at the assizes, but allowing him to proceed thither at his leisure, and in his own way, provided that he engaged to be there before the assizes commenced.

On the 2nd of April, accordingly, he was brought before Judge Turner, his old adversary, who, however, was now disposed to treat him more leniently than before, and would probably have released him, had it not been for a second interposition of Justice Parker, who was unwilling that he should be discharged, lest he himself should be said to have committed him to prison unjustly. He was in consequence sent back to remain a prisoner till the sessions, but with liberty, on the intercession of some other justices, to walk about the town.

·At the sessions the chairman was Judge Street, one of the judges on the Welsh circuit. When the indictment was read, which charged George, in addition to other offences, with having held a meeting at Tredington, to the terror of the king's subjects, he made various objections to it, and said, indeed, that it was a bundle of lies, and was moreover incorrect in form. The jury, however, gave a verdict against him; but he was allowed to find bail to appear at the next assizes, and even the gaoler's son offered to be surety for him. But with this indulgence he would not comply, as it would have been in some degree an acknowledgment of the justice of the proceedings against him. He was at last left at large, on giving his word to appear at the next sessions.

During his interval of liberty he visited London, and attended a great yearly meeting of the Quakers there. In the course of the proceedings, also, he heard of the death of his mother, at a very advanced age.

His next appearance at the sessions ended, like the others, in a remand to prison. While he was in confinement he was visited by the Earl of Salisbury's son, who made a list of the errors that were in the indictment, and a statement of his case was laid before Judge Wild; but the judge, on perusing it, merely observed that if they wished to try the validity of the indictment, they might try it. Before this time George had been joined by his wife, who, in despair, went up to London to intercede for him, and obtained an interview with the king. The king said that he would leave the matter to the chancellor, Lord Finch, to whom she accordingly went, and who told her that her husband could not be released unless by a pardon from the king. To this mode of release George would not consent, refusing to have it said that he was pardoned when he had done no wrong, and desiring merely to have the validity of his indictment tried before the Court of King's Bench. At length another *habeas corpus* was sent down to Worcester for his removal to London, whither, being ill and weak, he was conveyed in a coach the under-sheriff and the clerk of the peace accompanying him.

Previously to his appearance before the judges, he had secured the assistance of Mr. Corbet, a very able barrister, who had been recommended to him by some of his, or his wife's, friends. George, it will be recollected, had been kept in prison under the statute of *præmunire*, for having refused to take the oaths of allegiance and supremacy; Corbet argued that no man could be imprisoned under that statute, and the judges, after some demur, admitted that he was right. Corbet then adverted to the errors in the indictment, which he proved to be so many and so gross that the judges decided it should be quashed, and that George might have his liberty. But it happened that on that day several noblemen and other eminent persons were called upon to take the oaths of allegiance and supremacy in the court; and some of George's adversaries moved the judges that the oaths should be tendered to him again, observing that he was a dangerous man to be at large. But Hale, who was then Lord Chief Justice, said that he had indeed heard some such reports of George Fox, but that he had heard more good reports of him, and that he would therefore, with the concurrence of the other judges, order him to be set at liberty. "Thus," says George's journal, "after I had suffered imprisonment a year and almost two months for nothing, I was fairly set at liberty upon a trial of the errors in my indictment, without receiving any pardon or coming under any obligation or engagement at all. Counsellor Corbet, who pleaded for me, got great fame by it; for many of the lawyers came to him, and told him he had brought that to light which had not been known before, as to the not imprisoning on a *præmunire;* and after the trial a judge said to him, ' You have attained a great deal of honour by pleading George Fox's cause in court.' "

During his imprisonment at Worcester he had not been idle, but had sent forth a number of pamphlets and epistles. After being present at a few meetings in different parts, he went to Swarthmore, where he remained quiet for some time to recruit his health, amusing himself with writing small tracts, and making collections of papers issued by himself or his partisans.

He had to lament that many, who had

embraced his doctrine at first, had fallen off, and that some of them had done his party more mischief than those who had openly opposed it from the beginning.

CHAPTER XXVI.

George Fox visits Holland in company with Penn
and Barclay—His return—His letters to the King
of Poland, to the Grand Turk, and the Dey of
Algiers—Is sued for tithes—His second visit to
Holland—His letter to the Duke of Holstein respecting the liberty of women to speak to congregations—Several Quakers released from prison in
England—George Fox's last illness and death—
His character and personal appearance—Remarks
on Barclay's Apology—General observations regarding the Quakers.

In the early part of the year 1677, George
Fox, being now in the fifty-third year of his
age, resumed his travels through the country.
But it was not long before "it was upon
him" to go to Holland, to visit the Friends
there, and to promote the spread of his
doctrines in Germany.

He was accompanied in this journey by William Penn, Robert Barclay, Isabel Yeomans, one of his wife's daughters, and two or three other persons. They landed at Rotterdam.

Quakerism had made great progress in Holland, so that numerous meetings were held ; and Benjamin Furly, an English settler in Holland, and John Claus, a Quaker from Amsterdam, interpreted whatever any of the English felt moved to say. In a short time Penn and Barclay started for Germany, leaving George at Amsterdam, and taking Furly with them as interpreter.

Barclay had been in Germany before, and had had an interview, in the year preceding, with the Princess Elizabeth, daughter of Frederick, King of Bohemia, and sister of Sophia of Hanover, mother of George I., when the princess had expressed herself very favourably towards the Quakers. In consequence, George Fox, who was always ready enough to write letters to anybody, addressed to her an epistle from Amsterdam, to which she returned a courteous answer. This gave occasion to Barclay and Penn to wait on the princess at her residence near Paderborn, where they were well received, were allowed to hold a meeting, and afterwards invited to sup with the princess.

As to George Fox's travels in Holland and Westphalia, his account of them is but a mere catalogue of movements from place to place, with a few notices of meetings, and disputes with Baptists and others, at which John Claus acted as interpreter.

The party did not all return together. Barclay and George's daughter-in-law came back before George, who, with William Penn and some others, landed at Harwich on the 23rd of October, 1677.

From this period the life of George Fox presents but little variety of incident for the biographer. When he was sufficiently strong, he employed himself, as before, in travelling from town to town, and holding meetings; when he was ill or weak, he remained stationary, writing letters of exhortation to Friends, and others, at home and abroad. His wife was sometimes with him, but more frequently absent from him.

In 1678 he addressed a letter to John III., King of Poland, requesting that the Friends, being a peaceable people, might have liberty to conduct their religious worship, throughout his dominions, in their own way. In this epistle he quotes Augustin, Irenæus, Erasmus, and other authors whom he was incapable of reading, and names some of whom few have heard, as "Veritus" and "Retnaldus." Barclay may have helped him to some of his learning. He heard, by some means, that this letter reached the King of Poland, and was read by him; but it seems to have produced little effect, for six years afterwards George learned that there was still persecution in Poland, and wrote His Majesty another letter, in which, however, he confined himself to quotations from the Scripture. The second missile was probably as much of a *telum imbelle* as the first.

But the King of Poland was not the only ruler that called for George's admonition; the Great Turk and the Dey of Algiers required also to be exhorted. He wrote to the Great Turk, urging him to turn himself and his people from wickedness, lest they should be utterly destroyed; and to the. Dey of Algiers, requesting him to be less cruel to the Friends and others whom he held in captivity.

Looking at home, he wrote an address to all rulers and magistrates, beseeching them to be tolerant towards all dissenters, and to abstain from persecution.

In 1681 he and his wife were sued for tithes in Lancashire, but, as they demurred to the jurisdiction of the court, the cause was carried before the Court of Exchequer. After a long time spent in proceedings, a sequestration was issued against them both; but, by advice of counsel, they moved for a limitation, which in some degree disappointed the expectations of their adversaries, as it prevented more from being taken than could be proved. On this occasion, "one of the judges," says George, "was very bitter, and broke forth in a great rage against me in the open court; but in a little time after he died." This is not the only instance in which George insinuates that judgments have fallen upon men for acting against him: he does not assert the fact positively, but gives us to understand that we should be wrong in not inferring it.

During the latter part of his life he appears to have been but little molested by the authorities, who, indeed, seem to have at length left the Quakers very much to themselves. Sometimes soldiers, for the

sake of preventing disturbance, were sta-
tioned at the doors of meeting-houses,
or at other places, to prevent the Friends
from assembling; sometimes constables
showed unwillingness to act; sometimes
the justices, when Friends were brought
before them, deferred signing the warrant
for their commitment till another day, and
at last omitted to sign it at all.

In 1684 he felt "drawings in his spirit"
to make another visit to Holland, where he
passed between two and three months,
travelling about as on the former occasion.

Hearing that the Duke of Holstein had
expelled the Quakers from Frederickstadt
because they allowed women to speak in
their congregations, George wrote him a
letter filled with arguments in favour of
permitting women to speak in religious
assemblies. He reasons thus:

The text, "Let your women keep silence
in the churches, for it is not permitted

unto them to speak; but they are commanded to be under obedience, as also saith the law; and, if they will learn anything, let them ask their husbands at home, for it is a shame for women to speak in the church" (1 Cor. xiv. 34), is to be compared with the admonition to Timothy (1 Tim. ii. 11), "Let the woman learn in silence with all subjection; but I suffer not a woman to teach, nor to usurp authority over the man, but to be in silence;" and we shall then, says George, see what sort of women they are that the apostle intended to be in silence and subjection,—not all women, but such as sought to usurp authority over the man, that is, unruly women. To this he adds that there were prophetesses among the Jews, and that prophetesses must have spoken in public; that Moses wished that all the Lord's people were prophets, and that the Lord's people consisted of women as well as men; and that as to women asking their husbands at home, the unmarried and widows have no husbands, and the precept in their case is nugatory.

In 1686 the king, on repeated applications respecting such of the Quakers as were still in prison, issued an order for the release of all prisoners that were confined for conscience' sake; an event which caused great joy among the Friends, and which was celebrated by a large meeting in London in the early part of the year. Some, however, still continued in prison for refusing to pay tithes.

George Fox continued his labours till debility obliged him to relinquish them. He had never wholly recovered from the effects of his long imprisonment, and, during the latter years of his life, gradually grew weaker and weaker, till, on the evening of the 13th of November, 1690, he died, in great tranquillity, at the house of a Quaker named Henry Gouldney, in Whitehart Court, after having addressed a congregation, in the early part of the day, at the meeting-house in Gracechurch Street.

A man whose words made so much impression on those about him, and who was able to attract so many followers with so much ease, must have been possessed of a considerable portion of intellect. He had much acuteness, and some cunning, as was shown in his readiness to take advantage of any legal technicality at his appearances before magistrates and judges. He may be said to have had no learning, except of a scriptural kind, and being illuminated, as he professed, by the light of the Spirit, he affected to despise all human instruction and study of language; yet he was willing to make it appear, at times, that his reading had been much more extensive than it was, as in his letter to the King of Poland, and in the share which he allowed to be attributed to him in the "Battledore." His discourses to congregations were often rambling and incoherent; but there must have been some attraction about the manner of their delivery.

His written addresses and letters are filled with texts, and abound with repetitions. "In these compositions," says Croese, "he showed no great strength of language or thought; he wrote such characters as were not easy to be read, and expressed himself in so rude and simple a style, sometimes most difficult and intricate, that it is a wonder that any man, so much exercised in speaking and discussing, should have been the author of what proceeded from his pen."

"He left many books," says the same writer, "which some of his followers praise but faintly, while others extol them to the skies; but few touch them that are not of the Quakers' persuasion, and nobody reads them that loathes repetition of the same thing, in various dress of words and expressions, or dislikes the treatment of a subject with such prolixity as regards not what is sufficient, but how much can be said."

He provided by his will that his journal should be printed, and a copy of it sent to all the yearly and quarterly meetings of his followers throughout the world, as far as should be practicable. It is said to have undergone some revision, to put a little more grammar into its pages, before it went to press.

He was tall in stature, and of a large and strong frame, able to bear much fatigue and want of sleep, and was very moderate in eating and drinking. His activity, in the more vigorous part of his life, was great; he travelled from place to place among his people, as if he were desirous to be omnipresent, and thought nothing done rightly which he himself did not direct. How excessive was his obstinacy and power of endurance has been fully shown in the detail of his life.

His converts, however, with the exception of Penn and Barclay, were mostly of the humbler and more illiterate classes of mankind. Penn, as is well known, was the son of Admiral Sir William Penn, the friend of James II.; and his life has been copiously related by Clarkson. Of Barclay, though his "Apology for the Quakers," written by himself in Latin and in English, has been several times reprinted, much less is known. He was the son of David Barclay, of Ury, near Aberdeen, and, after receiving the rudiments of education among the Calvinists in his native country, was sent to Paris to continue his studies under his uncle, who was president of the Scotch college there. He made rapid progress, and resisted all attempts of the Papists to make him a proselyte. Returning home when he was little more than sixteen, in the year 1664, he found that his father had attached himself to the Quakers, and, as he himself liked their doctrine, he proceeded without hesitation to tread in his father's steps.

His Apology has been praised, and with justice, for the clearness and soundness of its reasoning: even Voltaire allows that it is as well drawn up as the subject could possibly admit. But all his reasoning is built upon an unsound principle. George Fox professed to be directed by an inward light or illumination of the mind. The guidance of this light Barclay begins his book by endeavouring to establish and vindicate, making it perfect and sufficient in itself, and amenable to no test or tribunal. "These divine inward revelations," says he, "which we make absolutely necessary for the building up of true faith, neither do nor can ever contradict the outward testimony of the Scriptures, or right and sound reason. Yet from hence it will not follow that these divine revelations are to be subjected to the examination, either of the outward testimony of the Scriptures, or of the natural reason of man, as to a more noble or certain rule or touchstone; for this divine revelation, and inward illumination, is that which is evident and clear of itself, forcing, by its own evidence and clearness, the well-disposed understanding to assent, irresistibly moving the same thereunto, even as the common principles of natural truth move and incline the mind to a natural assent." It is wonderful that a man who could reason so well should have begun with premises so utterly fallacious. These divine illuminations, he says, will never contradict sound reason, yet are not to be referred to the decision of reason; but how is it to be known whether they contradict sound reason or not, except by referring them to the decision of reason?

The other propositions which we find set forth in Barclay's book are in entire accordance with what was preached by George Fox: that man fell; that Christ died for all men, and vouchsafes to every man a portion of light, by which, if it is not resisted, he may obtain salvation. Christ's atonement is therefore universal, and even the heathen may be saved by it, since Christ was sent as *a light to lighten the Gentiles*, and the heathen may profit by his light, if they do not resist it, even though they know not the means by which it is ministered to them, as men in disease may be cured by good remedies, even though they are ignorant who compounded them or whence they came. But those who knowingly resist the gift of this light render it their condemnation. As to the ministry, it is by the manifestation of this light that men are led to minister or become evangelists to others, and they are directed by it as to the times and places of their ministration, and the persons to whom they are to minister; they are to give freely as they have received freely, and are not to wait for any human commission or educa‐ tion; "yet if God has called any from their employments or trades, by which they ac‐ quire their livelihood, it may be lawful for such (according to the liberty which they feel given them in the Lord) to receive such temporal supplies as may be needful to them for meat or clothing, and as may be freely given them by those to whom they have communicated spiritual supplies."

As to religious worship, it must be spon‐ taneous and immediate, and consequently all prescribed forms of prayer or praise are mere empty superstitions. As to baptism, it must be spiritual, the baptism of John having been appointed only for a time, as a figure of inward newness of life, and the baptism of infants being a mere human practice, for which no precept or authority is to be found in the Scripture. As to the eucharist, it was also figurative, or a shadow of divine nourishment in the heart, which shadow need not be regarded by those who have received the substance.

To establish the doctrine of the internal light, Barclay interprets the words δι' αὐτοῦ in the seventh verse of the first chapter of St. John, not "through him," as we render them, but "through it," that is, through the light, referring αὐτοῦ to φωτός, the substantive nearest to it. If the propriety of this interpretation be granted, it will serve the Quakers but little.

In a passage worthy of George Fox himself, Barclay tells us why the Quakers were raised up among mankind. "It is from a sense of their blindness and ignorance," says he, " that has come over Christendom, that we, the Friends, are led and moved of the Lord so constantly and frequently to call all, invite all, request all, to turn to the light in them, to mind the light in them, to believe in Christ as He is in them; and that in the name, power, and authority of the Lord, not in school arguments and distinctions (for which many of the wise men of this world account us fools and madmen), but we do charge and command them to lay aside their wisdom, to come down out of that proud, airy brain knowledge, and to stop that mouth, how eloquent soever to the worldly ear it may appear, and to be silent, and to sit down as in the dust, and to mind the light of Christ in their own consciences, which, if minded, they would find as a two-edged sword in their hearts, and as a fire and a hammer, that would knock against and burn up all that carnal, gathered, natural stuff,

P

and make the stoutest of them all tremble, and become Quakers indeed. Which
those that come not to feel now, and kiss
the Son while the day lasteth, but harden
their hearts, will feel to be a certain truth
when it is too late. To conclude, as saith
the apostle, 'All ought to examine themselves, whether they be in the faith indeed,
and try their own selves; for except Jesus
Christ be in them, they are certainly repro-
bates.' "

The numbers of the Quakers, as has
been already observed, are not increasing,
but rather diminishing. Such must natu-
rally be the fate of Quakerism; it was spread
by effort for a time, but no efforts will secure
it unlimited extension, or prevent it from
decay. Human nature remains always the
same, and no large proportion of mankind
have ever shown a disposition to make themselves resemble the Quakers. Men are not
yet prepared to relinquish contention, to

submit to spoliation and personal violence, to abstain from law-suits, to abolish armies and navies, and to turn their spears into pruning-hooks. The world was intended to be as it is; and if peace were spread throughout it, it would be but a waste of dulness and inactivity, like that which is described in Goldsmith's tale of Asem the Hermit. However strictly the Quakers have adhered to their religious doctrines and tenets, many of them, in the distinctions of dress, and the furniture and decoration of their houses, have, in the present day, re-ceded far from the rules and practices of their forefathers. Their garments have be-come gradually more assimilated to those of other human beings; and their houses, which were to admit no pictures or statues, or useless ornamentation, have, in later times, been adorned, among the wealthier class, by the finest productions of art. These relaxations in the heads of families prepare the way for final defection in their descendants. The son sees his father grow daily more and more like the rest of the world, and is led to determine, as soon as he becomes his own master, to throw off all sectarian peculiarities, and to appear a man like other men. Deviations in smaller matters, too, lead to deviations in greater. The Quaker who has once begun to vary, in things which the world would call indifferent, from his fellows, is ready to ask himself how he would be injured if he should vary from them in things of apparently more importance. If it be well with the majority of those around me who differ in creed and ceremonies from the Quakers, why may it not be well with me, he will say, if I desert the creed and ceremonies of the Quakers, and adopt those of the majority around me?

Of learning there has been among the Quakers but little. Barclay is almost the only scholar that they have had; though

Penn, indeed, had some scholarship, and Keith, who, however, can scarcely be called a Quaker, had probably as much. Nor have any of them attained high places among mankind; they could not be captains, or lawyers, or clergymen, and little was left for them but trade, in which they have been on a level with other men. When any of the sect conceive a desire for learning, or grow ambitious of distinction, they soon cease to be Quakers.

THE END.

Woodfall and Kinder, Printers, Angel Court, Skinner Street, London.

Messrs. Saunders, Otley, and Co.'s
East India Army, Colonial,
and General Agency.
50, Conduit Street, Hanover Square, London.

(In the immediate vicinity of the New East India House and the Oriental Club.)

MESSRS. SAUNDERS, OTLEY, and Co. beg to announce that, in consequence of their daily increasing relations with India, Australia, and the Colonies, they have opened an East India Army, Colonial, and General Agency, in connection with their long-established Publishing House, and they take this opportunity to invite the attention of Regimental Messes, Officers, Members of the Civil Service, and other Residents in India, Australia, and the Colonies thereto, and to the advantages it offers.

Banking Department.

PAY, PENSIONS, FUND ALLOWANCES, DIVIDENDS, &c. drawn and remitted with regularity. SALES of, and INVESTMENTS in, Government Stock, Foreign Securities, &c. effected. Every other description of FINANCIAL BUSINESS transacted.

Supply Department.

MISCELLANEOUS SUPPLIES OF EVERY DESCRIPTION, including Provisions, Wines, Plate, Jewellery, Books, Guns, Band Instruments, Clothing, &c. carefully selected and despatched by Overland Route, or Sailing Ship, to Regiments, and Messes in India, Australia, and the Colonies.

PRIVATE ORDERS from Officers, Members of the Civil Service, and Residents in India, Australia, and the Colonies generally, are executed with care, economy, efficiency, and promptitude.

All orders should be accompanied by full and detailed directions.

Personal Agency Department.

The Constituents of Messrs. Saunders, Otley, and Co. may depend upon receiving every attention to their requirements and instructions. Every assistance will be afforded to their Constituents and their Families on their arrival in England, with the view to relieve them from every possible inconvenience.

Charge, when required, will be taken of children coming from India and the Colonies, and arrangements will be made for their education in England.

To those going out to India, Australia, and the Colonies, Messrs. Saunders, Otley, and Co. offer their services to secure passages Overland, or by Ship, and to afford them all necessary information connected therewith.

All Letters, Parcels, &c. will be received by Messrs. Saunders, Otley, and Co. for their Constituents (whether in England, India, or the Colonies), to whom they will be forwarded regularly.

Terms.

No COMMISSION CHARGED on the execution of Orders, whether from Regimental Messes or Private Individuals, WHEN ACCOMPANIED BY A REMITTANCE, and a small Discount at all times allowed.

The Oriental Budget of Literature,

for India, China, Auſtralia, and the Colonies,

PRICE THREE PENCE.

Annual Subſcription (including poſtage to any part of the world), 4s.

The "ORIENTAL BUDGET" may be ordered from Meſſrs. SAUNDERS, OTLEY,
& Co. direct, or through any of their local Agents. Subſcriptions
may be remitted in poſtage ſtamps.

The "ORIENTAL BUDGET" of Literature is a complete and perfect record of
the Literature of the Month, and will be found eminently uſeful and intereſting
to reſidents in India and the Colonies.

It contains Critical Notices of every New work of importance publiſhed in
the previous month, thus leading the diſtant reader, who has no other means of
aſcertaining the merits of new publications, to a diſcriminate purchaſe of books.

It contains valuable literary information and goſſip relating both to men and
books, Engliſh and Foreign; and its Literary Intelligence keeps the reader well
informed reſpecting all that takes place in the World of Letters.

It ſupplies a complete Liſt of the Publications of the Month—whilſt their
prices—the names of their Publiſhers—their Authors—are all accurately ſtated,
and the fulleſt information in reference to Works in the preſs is given.

Publiſhed on the 1ſt of every month, by
Meſſrs. SAUNDERS, OTLEY, & Co, 50, Conduit Street, Hanover Square, London.

Messrs. SAUNDERS, OTLEY, & Co.'s
LITERARY ANNOUNCEMENTS.

THE VOYAGE of the NOVARA;
The Austrian Expedition Round the World. With upwards of 400 steel and wood engravings.

THE LIFE AND WRITINGS of the RIGHT
HON. BENJAMIN DISRAELI, M.P.

THE LIFE OF GEORGE FOX,
The Founder of the Quakers.

THE TRAVELS AND ADVENTURES OF
DR. WOLFF, the Bokhara Missionary. Dedicated to the Right Hon. W. E. Gladstone, M.P. 1st. vol. 2d. edition. [2nd. vol. immediately.

THE PRIVATE JOURNAL
OF THE MARQUESS OF HASTINGS, Governor-General and Commander-in-Chief in India.
Edited by his Daughter, Sophia, the Marchioness of Bute. Second Edition, 2 vols. post 8vo, with Map and Index. 21s.

NAPOLEON THE THIRD ON ENGLAND.
Selections from his own writings. Translated by J. H. Simpson. 5s.

THE HUNTING GROUNDS of the OLD
WORLD. By H. A. L. (the Old Shekarry). Second Edition.

HIGHLANDS AND HIGHLANDERS;
As they were and as they are. By William Grant Stewart. First and Second series, price 5s. each; extra bound, 6s. 6d.

THE ENGLISHMAN IN CHINA.
With numerous Woodcuts.

AN AUTUMN TOUR IN SPAIN.
With numerous Engravings.

LECTURES ON THE EPISTLE TO THE
EPHESIANS. By the Rev. R. J. M'GHEE. Second Edition. 2 vols, Reduced price, 15s.

PRE-ADAMITE MAN; or,
THE STORY OF OUR OLD PLANET AND ITS INHABITANTS, TOLD BY SCRIPTURE AND SCIENCE. Beautifully Illustrated by Hervieu, Dalziel Brothers, &c. 1 vol, post 8vo, 10s. 6d.

LOUIS CHARLES DE BOURBON;
THE "PRISONER OF THE TEMPLE." 3s.

A HANDY-BOOK for RIFLE VOLUNTEERS.
With 14 Coloured Plates and Diagrams. By Captain W. G. Hartley, author of "A New System of Drill." 7s. 6d.

RECOLLECTIONS of a WINTER CAMPAIGN
IN INDIA, in 1857—58. By CAPTAIN OLIVER J. JONES, R.N. With numerous illustrations drawn on stone by Day, from the Author's Sketches. In 1 vol. royal 8vo, 16s.

TWO YEARS IN SYRIA.
Ry T. LEWIS FARLEY, Esq., Late Chief Accountant of the Ottoman Bank, Beyrout. 12s.

DIARY of TRAVELS in THREE QUARTERS
OF THE GLOBE. By an AUSTRALIAN SETTLER. 2 vols, post 8vo, 21s.

MOUNT LEBANON and its INHABITANTS:
A Ten Years' Residence from 1842 to 1852. By Colonel CHURCHILL, Staff Officer in the British Expedition to Syria. Second Edition. 3 vols, 8vo, £1 5s.

TRAVEL and RECOLLECTIONS of TRAVEL.
By Dr JOHN SHAW. 1 vol, post 8vo, 7s. 6d.

LETTERS ON INDIA.
By EDWARD SULLIVAN, Esq., Author of 'Rambles in North and South America;' 'The Bungalow and the Tent;' 'From Boulogne to Babel-Mandeb;' 'A Trip to the Trenches;' &c. 1 vol. 7s.

CAMPAIGNING IN KAFFIRLAND; or,
SCENES AND ADVENTURES IN THE KAFFIR WAR OF 1851—52. By Captain W. R. KING. Second Edition. 1 vol. 8vo, 14s.

Mrs. JAMESON'S LIVES OF FEMALE
SOVEREIGNS. Third Edition. 21s.

Mrs. JAMESON'S CHARACTERISTICS
OF WOMEN. New Library Edition. On Fine Tinted Paper, with illustrations from the Author's Designs. 2 vols. post 8vo, 21s.

ADVENTURES OF A GENTLEMAN
IN SEARCH OF A HORSE. By Sir George Stephen. With illustrations by Cruikshank. Sixth Edition, 7s. 6d.

Dispatch.—" Every one interested in horses should read this work."
Review.—" It is full of the most ludicrous adventures, coupled with soundest advice."

THE LANGUAGE OF FLOWERS,
Elegant Gift Book for the Season. Beautifully bound in green watered silk, with coloured plates. Containing the Art of Conveying Sentiments of Esteem and Affection.

> " By all those token flowers, which tell
> What words can never speak so well."—*Byron.*

Eleventh edition, dedicated, by permission, to the Duchess of Kent. 10s. 6d.

THE MANAGEMENT OF BEES;
With a description of the " Ladies' Safety Hive." By Samuel Bagster, Jun. 1 vol., illustrated. 7s.

THE HANDBOOK OF TURNING,
With numerous plates. A complete and Practical Guide to the Beautiful Science of Turning in all its Branches. 1 vol. 7s. 6d.

TEXTS FOR TALKERS.
By Frank Fowler.

THE NEWSPAPER PRESS OF THE
PRESENT DAY.

ARMY MISRULE; BARRACK THOUGHTS.
By a Common Soldier. 3s.

Fiction.

CRISPIN KEN; or,
PASSAGES FROM THE LIFE OF A CLERGYMAN. By the Author of ' Miriam May.' Dedicated, by permission, to the Rev. Joseph Wolff, D.D., L.L.D.

WHO SHALL BE DUCHESS? or,
THE NEW LORD OF BURLEIGH. A Novel. 2 vols., 21s.

THE LIGHTHOUSE. A Novel. 2 vols., 21s.

THE SKELETON IN THE CUPBOARD.
By Lady Scott. 2 vols.

TOO LATE.
By Mrs. Dimsdale.

WHY PAUL FERROLL KILLED HIS
WIFE. By the Author of Paul Ferroll.

HELEN. A Romance of Real Life.

GERTRUDE MELTON.

MY WIFE'S PINMONEY.
By E. E. Nelson.

THE EMIGRANT'S DAUGHTER.
Dedicated, by permission, to the Empress of Russia.

THE SENIOR FELLOW.

ALMACK'S.
A Novel. Dedicated to the Ladies Patronesses of the Balls at Almack's. 1 vol, crown 8vo, 10s. 6d.

NELLY CAREW.
By Miss Power. 2 vols, 21s.

MEMOIRS of a LADY IN WAITING.
By the Author of 'Adventures of Mrs. Colonel Somerset in Caffraria.' 2 vols, 18s.

HULSE HOUSE.
A Novel. By the Author of 'Anne Gray.' 2 vols. post 8vo, 21s.

THE NEVILLES OF GARRETSTOWN.
A Historical Tale. Edited, and with a Preface by the Author of 'Emilia Wyndham.' 3 vols, post 8vo, 31s. 6d.

CORVODA ABBEY.
A Tale. 1 vol, post 8vo, 10s. 6d.

THE VICAR OF LYSSEL.
The Diary of a Clergyman in the 18th century. 4s. 6d.

GOETHE IN STRASBOURG.
A Dramatic Nouvelette. By H. Noel Humphreys. 6s.

MIRIAM MAY.
A Romance of Real Life. Fourth Edition. 1 vol., 10s. 6d.

ROTTEN ROW. A Novel.

SQUIRES AND PARSONS.
A Church Novel. 1 vol. 10s. 6d.

THE DEAN; or, the POPULAR PREACHER.
By BERKELEY AIKIN, Author of 'Anne Sherwood.' 3 vols. post 8vo, 31s. 6d.

CHARLEY NUGENT; or,
PASSAGES IN THE LIFE OF A SUB. A Novel, 3 vols, post 8vo, 31s. 6d.

PAUL FERROLL.
By the Author of 'IX Poems by V.' Fourth Edition. Post 8vo, 10s. 6d.

LADY AUBREY; or,
WHAT SHALL I DO? By the Author of 'Every Day.' A Novel. 2 vols., 21s.

THE IRONSIDES.
A Tale of the English Commonwealth.

AGNES HOME.

Poetry.

Sir E. L. Bulwer's Eva,
AND OTHER POEMS.

Earl Godwin's Feast,
AND OTHER POEMS.   By Stewart Lockyer.

Saint Bartholomew's Day,
AND OTHER POEMS.   By Stewart Lockyer.

Sacred Poems.
By the late Right Hon. Sir Robert Grant, with a Notice by Lord Glenelg.

Eustace ;
An Elegy.   By the Right Hon. Charles Tennyson D'Eyncourt.

The Pleasures of Home.
By the Rev. J. T. Campbell.

Friendship ;
AND OTHER POEMS.   By HIBERNICUS.   5s.

Judith ;
AND OTHER POEMS.   By FRANCIS MILLS, M.R.C.S.L.   5s.

The Convert,
AND OTHER POEMS.   5s.

The Progress of Truth.
A Fragment of a Sacred Poem.

Alzim ; or, the Way to Happiness.
By Edwin W. Simcox.

Oberon's Empire.
A Mask.

The Spirit of Home.
By Sylvan.

The Moslem and the Hindoo.
A Poem on the Sepoy Revolt.   By a Graduate of Oxford.

Melancholy,
AND OTHER POEMS.   Second Edition.   By Thomas Cox.

Reliquiæ:
Poems. By Edward Smith.

Palmam, qui Meruit, Ferat.
By Norman B. Yonge.

Miscellaneous Poems.
By an Indian Officer.

The Shadow of the Yew,
AND OTHER POEMS. By Norman B. Yonge.

Carmagnola.
An Italian Tale of the Fifteenth Century.

Hanno.
A Tragedy. The Second Edition.

War Lyrics.
Second Edition. By A. and L. Shore.

British and Foreign Public Library,

For Authors Publishing.

www.ingramcontent.com/pod-product-compliance
Lightning Source LLC
Chambersburg PA
CBHW031141120726
47905CB00006B/1768